The
Collision

The
Collision

The Impact Series

C K Westbrook

CK Westbrook

7-17-23

4 Horsemen
Publications, Inc.

4 Horsemen
Publications, Inc.

4 Horsemen Publications, Inc.
1497 Main St. Suite 169
Dunedin, FL 34698
4horsemenpublications.com
info@4horsemenpublications.com

Typesetting by Niki Tantillo
Edited by Heather Teele

Library of Congress Control Number: 2022938512

Paperback ISBN-13: 978-1-64450-622-6
EBook ISBN-13: 978-1-64450-621-9
Audiobook ISBN-13: 978-1-64450-620-2

For Karen

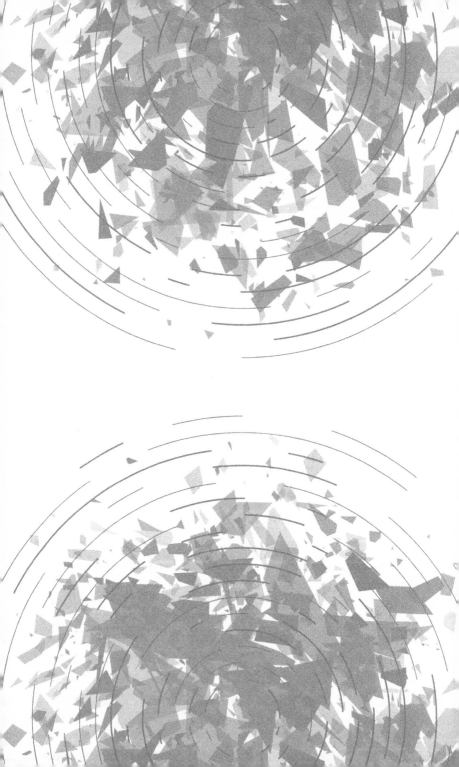

ACKNOWLEDGEMENTS

I want to thank 4 Horsemen Publications for their continued support of me and this series. Val, Jen, Erika, and Heather have made this complicated, and a little daunting, process smooth and fulfilling. I want to thank Chelsea for her constant friendship, insider knowledge, and brilliant editing skills. Chelsea understands Kate, Sinclair, and Kyle as well as I do, and these novels would not exist without her. I also want to thank Denise for her supportive friendship and for sharing her vast knowledge of space exploration and its community. I am grateful to my sisters, Shana and Jess, for their encouragement and love. I need to thank my silent writing partners, Skye and Bruichladdich, for always being close. This series would have remained just a daydream without Jeffrey's encouragement, patience, and love; I am forever grateful for him. Lastly, my most profound appreciation goes to my readers. I am extremely thankful to every person who read *The Shooting*, especially those who said they could not wait to read the next book!

Table of Contents

ONE

Forty-Eight Days After the Shooting

Several hundred feet to the right, something fell from the sky with such force that it bounced, shaking the ground and the car.

Sinclair instinctively jerked the car left into the oncoming traffic lane; luckily, the next car coming toward them was far enough away to hit their brakes, avoiding an accident. Sinclair regained control, pulling to the right, hitting the brakes, and swerving onto the shoulder before coming to an abrupt halt.

"What the fuck?" Sinclair shouted as he watched it bounce again, moving closer to the highway.

"Drive! Why are you stopping!" Kate screamed as she frantically looked up to the sky. "There could be more!"

But he did not move. Sinclair, breathing hard, stared in the direction of the object as it settled in a field on the side of the road.

"What was that?" Sinclair asked as he opened the car door.

Kate got out as well, glancing at two other cars which had come to loud, screeching halts on the highway. She was thankful that there were so few cars on the road, so there was no chain reaction pile-up.

"This is crazy, Sinclair. We should go!" Kate said, looking toward the object.

Her heart pounded madly as Sinclair stepped over the guardrail and walked through a little ditch into the field.

Why does he need to see what almost killed us?

But she was curious, so she watched as he walked to a wire fence not visible from the road.

Kate followed him slowly.

"I know what it is, but I don't believe my own eyes," Sinclair said as Kate approached.

"Is it a car?" Kate asked.

"Yes, I think it's a Tesla Roadster," Sinclair replied, staring at the smashed object.

"I love electric cars, but not when they almost kill me! Where did it come from?" Kate asked confusedly. She looked around and up at the sky. "There is nothing high enough here to explain where it came from."

"I think it was on its way to the asteroid belt. On its way to Mars, Kate. It fell from space. It's not possible to be this intact; it should have exploded, disintegrated," Sinclair said, staring at the car and shaking his head.

Kate's stomach sank. "It's Rex; this is some kind of warning."

TWO

Forty-Eight Days After the Shooting

Earlier that day

Kate's head bobbed back and forth until she finally gave in to sleep. She usually loved sleeping in cars, but dreams of nuclear bombs and mushroom clouds snapped her awake. She saw flashes of movies about dystopian life after a nuclear war. Sighing loudly, she opened her eyes.

"Are we there yet?" she asked Sinclair in a whiny, childish voice, trying to lighten the mood after all they'd gone through during the last 24 hours. Her tactic didn't work though; her eyes scanned the horizon for an explosion or unnatural cloud.

It would be just my luck that this day would be capped off with a nuclear holocaust.

"We'll be there soon," Sinclair said without taking his eyes off the road.

Kate hoped his instincts were right; she was putting all her faith in him.

"I've been thinking: what items did you bring?" he asked.

She didn't exactly have time to pack when she ran away from that terrifying and violent mob this morning, jumping into Sinclair's car for safety and fleeing Washington D.C.

"Just my phone and this mask," Kate responded, waving her green *"Vegan for Life"* mask. It was dirty and crumpled from being smashed in the pocket of her shorts. "Wish I'd grabbed a clean one. Shoot, I don't even have my ID."

How long will we be gone?

"That's okay. I'm driving. We need to stop and get supplies. I don't want people to recognize you," Sinclair said, turning the car into a strip mall with both a pharmacy and grocery store.

Kate couldn't shake the nuclear dream; hopefully, it wasn't an omen of things to come. "Do you know if there are nuclear bombs everywhere or just out West? Are they all in underground bunkers, or are some on military bases throughout the country?"

"Not sure about military bases. I bet there are some on the ships near Norfolk not far from here. Why?" Sinclair asked, sounding concerned.

"No real reason; I just had a nightmare," Kate replied, looking over her shoulder through the back window.

Because of the pandemic and the July 14th shootings, the parking lot, which normally would have been busy on a Monday afternoon, was barely a quarter full.

The mass shooting that led everyone in possession of a gun to turn it on themselves was like a deranged rapture of gun owners. Around the same time, on the same day, more than seventy million Americans killed themselves; worldwide, it was hundreds of millions. Amid the fear and panic, most people were staying home.

Sinclair parked near the entrance of the Target and picked up Yvette's phone. It was apparent to Kate that he still missed Yvette. Since Yvette's suicide during the mass shooting, Sinclair had been reaching out to her contacts. He scrolled for a number and dialed. The phone was on speaker, and Sinclair looked at Kate, putting a finger to his mouth indicating her silence.

"Hello?" a woman answered, sounding suspicious.

"Hi, is this Dr. Claudia Chen?" Sinclair asked.

"Yes. Sinclair Jones?" the woman asked, sounding relieved.

"Hi, Claudia. Yes, it's me. How are you? I have been meaning to reach out. So sorry for your loss, losses," Sinclair said.

"And the same to you," the woman responded with a sigh. "It's been a terrible year. Unfathomable. How do we go on? So much loss. I wish I could talk to Yvette about it. Oh, how I miss her."

Kate still couldn't believe that Yvette had been a gun owner, that she was gone.

"Same here. Every day. I know you two were very close," Sinclair said.

They were both quiet for a moment.

"Claudia, are you still working at Wallops?" Sinclair asked.

"Yes. I'm here now. I come in a few days a week. I prefer it to working from home. The house is too empty; this place is pretty empty, too. Most staff work from home because of the virus and the shooting. Guess I am adhering to Yvette's life motto: 'Best way to be happy is to throw yourself into your work and forget about everything else.' Right, Sinclair? What was it she used to say? It was something like that. I would always laugh because it seemed kind of extreme, but Yvette was an intense woman. I loved that about her, so much passion for her work."

Sinclair flinched before responding, "Yvette loved her work. She often said it was her true love."

So, Yvette was a workaholic? No wonder they were struggling with their marriage before the shooting.

"Listen, Claudia, I'm in your neck of the woods right now. I was hoping I could stop by to talk," he said, raising an eyebrow at Kate.

"Oh, okay. Why don't you come here to Wallops?" Claudia replied.

"I was hoping to meet at your house or someplace outside. Is there a park nearby? It's a beautiful day and outdoors may be safer with the virus," he responded.

"Sure. Of course. There is a little park next to a dog park about a mile from my house. I'll text you the name so you can find it. I need to wrap up a few things here, but I'll meet you there in an hour, okay?" Claudia asked.

"Perfect. Thank you. See you soon," Sinclair said before hanging up. He turned quickly to Kate. "Okay,

now we get you a disguise. You need to hear what
Claudia says, but she must not recognize you as the
person of interest in the shooting now that those assholes at Space Force are trying to make you the scapegoat. I'm sure Claudia watches the news and has seen
your picture." Sinclair got out of the car and handed
Kate some cash.

The store was empty as Kate shopped; not a
single person was in the store except for the cashier.
It reminded Kate of the dystopian dreams she was
having earlier. She wanted to finish fast and get out
of this ominous, sad place.

Fifteen minutes later, they met back at the car.
Kate had bought a few cheerful masks with flowers
and rainbows. She also bought cheap, cute sunglasses
and a reusable water bottle. She considered the hats,
but they all looked too new. She didn't want to seem
obvious in trying to disguise herself.

"You look the exact same, Kate," Sinclair said with
a laugh. He bought hand sanitizer, fruit, chips, water,
and a few bottles of iced tea. He rummaged in his
trunk and pulled out a beat-up Nationals baseball cap.

Kate readjusted the hat size and pulled her hair
back through the hole, making her long, wavy brown
hair less obvious. She checked out her reflection
in the car window. She looked like a teenager. She
never looked her age of twenty-seven anyway; she
was carded all the time, and people often asked what
school she attended. The mask covered her distinctive
full lips, and until the past year, big smile.

"I think this is good, Sinclair. We can't see my char-
acteristics, and it doesn't look like I'm trying to hide."

"You look young, so I'll introduce you as Katie, Yvette's special intern. Meaning, like Yvette, you worked for both corporate and NASA. Claudia knows about Yvette's side gigs. If she thinks we all know, she'll be more forthcoming. I hope so anyway, or this could be a useless trip," Sinclair said.

Kate jumped at a loud screech and explosion just 100 feet behind them. She covered her ears and instinctively squatted down. A person across the parking lot screamed.

"Jesus Christ! What the hell?" Sinclair spun around toward the noise. "Never mind. It was only a car accident, Kate. Yep, just two cars. Just a normal fender bender," Sinclair said, searching up and down the street, turning around to be sure his words were true. He reached down and helped Kate stand. "See, just two cars. No violence, well except to those cars," he said in a soothing voice that had the opposite effect on her nerves. Kate felt even more jittery and on edge. "Even in a pandemic, people drive like morons."

THREE

Forty-Eight Days After the Shooting

When they arrived at the park, they scouted a picnic table close to a big oak tree. The tree provided shade, but the occasional breeze allowed the sun to shine through the branches. Keeping their sunglasses on would seem natural, and the table was small enough that masks were needed.

"What time is it?" Kate asked Sinclair. "It's strange to think the day started with someone shattering my front window."

"Not even 2:30. It's been a long day," Sinclair said, getting out the iced teas and snacks. "Here she comes." He looked over Kate's shoulder to the parking area. He stood up and waved so Claudia would see them.

"Sinclair! So good to see you! I want to give you a tight hug, but I don't dare. There has been too much COVID in my life already," Claudia said as she sat down.

"It's great seeing you, Claudia. Thanks for cutting out of work and meeting us. I want to introduce Katie to you. She was a very special intern, really an assistant of Yvette's. She worked with Yvette on several of her projects."

"Oh, I see. Nice to meet you, Katie, and sorry for your loss as well. If you worked with Yvette, you knew how passionate and intense she was about her projects. It was so unfortunate that she was home with her gun, considering how much she traveled for work. Back and forth to Texas, California, and Florida, all the time. I wish she hadn't been in D.C. on July 14. Of course, I am sure you both feel the same, especially you Sinclair," Claudia said, reaching for his hand across the table. "Oh, sorry. Maternal instinct, touching people."

"I wish she had gotten rid of that revolver. She hadn't taken it out of the box in years." Sinclair's voice sounded thick, like he was holding back tears. Claudia squeezed both his hands, succumbing to her instincts to comfort.

"We all miss her so much," Claudia said with a sigh. "So, what are you doing here? I could see a road trip remembrance to celebrate Yvette's life if we weren't living in such deadly times. Since Katie is with you, I assume this is about work."

"Do you want an iced tea or snack?" Sinclair said, handing her a bottle and opening the chips. He also put hand sanitizer on the table. "Yes. We are here to ask about Yvette's work, specifically, her research about that big explosion last year."

Kate remembered sitting in Rock Creek Park after being questioned by Space Force when Sinclair told her about the big collision and Yvette's strange behavior. That was when she realized Sinclair genuinely believed her about Rex and was willing to help her. Here he was now, still helping her, trying to figure out if that explosion had anything to do with Rex.

Sinclair continued, "The one that was all over the news. Yvette was obsessed with it. I was only somewhat concerned because I knew you all at NASA and Yvette would find out what caused it. The A-team was involved and would solve the mystery. I also knew Yvette and NASA would let me know if anything pertinent to my research was discovered, but it just seemed to disappear from the media. Yvette was still working and traveling even as the pandemic shut everything down. I assumed she was researching the collision. After she died, and I was stuck in the house with my memories, I started digging through her work. Yvette had copious notes from the impact and research. She did a lot of process of elimination and seemed to have determined what was *not* involved."

Sinclair paused and Claudia jumped in. "The first few days everyone was trying to determine if their equipment was damaged. As an astrophysicist, I was intrigued, but Yvette was consumed with calculating damage. Yvette was working overtime, checking on NASA satellites and interests, as well as corporate concerns. Everyone was freaking out because the collision was enormous. Once it was determined that nothing of ours was destroyed in the immediate explosion, we were all monitoring the trajectory of the debris. Would it set off a chain reaction of collisions? Some of Yvette's clients were upset. They couldn't afford to lose their satellites, either because a big sports event was coming up or they needed information; some might say spying. NASA was concerned about its satellites and the International Space Station. The Department of Defense and Space Force was in a panic. It was all-hands-on-deck for weeks. Stressful and interesting times. A preamble to these days," Claudia paused and took a long sip of tea.

Kate could see all of Claudia's face when she lowered her mask to drink and decided she would not drink or eat anything.

"Anyway, it was crazy. And then it all went quiet. I just assumed everyone was taking a long breath of relief. No real damage, financially or politically. No deadly chain reaction. Everyone, government agencies, politicians, and corporate space, was relieved. If you think about it, it could have been a colossal problem. Ricocheted materials could have been devastating. NASA and the world dodged a bullet. Yvette continued her research tracking the debris using our equipment and equipment in Texas, Florida, and Hawaii. She was communicating with international interests. She was determined to find out exactly what happened. I didn't know who she was working for at that point, but she was obsessed. She would come here, use my office, sleep in my spare room, and we barely spoke. She seemed motivated as she always was, so I didn't think much of it. While it may have been a little extreme, I remembered that the pandemic was affecting everyone in different ways. I figured we would have margaritas when she cracked it. Is what she found on her computer?" Claudia asked.

"I looked as best I can. Some information is encrypted, you know, depending on who she was billing. I can see the research but not the raw data and conclusion. I will keep trying. Will you dig around here? See if she left anything that could be helpful?" Sinclair asked.

"I'm happy to help. Breaking rules doesn't matter anymore. We are in Armageddon now, and I am a scientist saying that!" Claudia said, laughing in a slightly hysterical way. "I lost my dad to COVID in April. I lost both my sons and my ex in the shooting. What can NASA do to me? Fire me? For going through Yvette's files? Maybe I should sell them to one of her clients?" Claudia said, nodding at Kate.

Oh, she must think I am representing Yvette's corporate clients. That's good.

Under the mask and behind her new sunglasses, she let tears roll down her face.

How could Claudia sustain so much pain?

Kate sobbed as both Claudia and Sinclair looked at her.

"Sorry, but I did not know. I am so sorry for all your loss. My heart is breaking for you," Kate said as another little sob escaped.

Claudia shrugged. "What can I do? I moved here after my dissertation. Married a local boy. Bill hunted his whole life and had lots of guns. My boys grew up hunting and shooting. I appreciated that they were self-sufficient. They were strong, rugged men and could feed themselves if necessary. My youngest left college and moved back home when the campus shut down due to the virus. I thought he would be safe here." Claudia broke down and just wailed.

Sinclair took both her hands and attempted to console her. "I am so, so sorry, Claudia. They loved you so much. It's so much loss."

Kate wanted to hug her; she balled her hands into fists to stop herself. The tears continued to stream down her face behind her glasses and mask.

"My eldest was in Richmond in his recently purchased townhouse. He was an engineer for the city. Starting his life. He had a great boyfriend. We all thought he was the one. Maybe a wedding soon. I thought he was safe as well. Safe at his home during a pandemic. Both my boys safe in their homes with their guns," Claudia continued between sobs.

Kate moved closer to Claudia and was rubbing her back. It wasn't as good as a hug, but Kate knew she needed kindness and human contact.

Claudia sighed and took a deep breath. "At first, I blamed Bill. He gave them the guns. Made my boys love guns. I'm from Hong Kong. Moved to Los Angeles as a child. My parents were professors. I never even held a gun until I started to date Bill. I thought when in Rome, or southern Virginia, do as the rednecks do. I adopted my community ways. Though I never bought a gun; I never had the desire. I figured that was something for the boys to do together." Claudia paused and took a sip of tea, composing herself. "I don't blame Bill anymore. I blame that fucking bitch who works for Space Force and knows what caused this mass murder," Claudia said, pure venom in her voice.

FOUR

Forty-Eight Days After the Shooting

K ate's hand abruptly stopped rubbing Claire's back, and her eyes flew to Sinclair.

"She knows what happened and won't tell us. Is she covering for someone? Did she do it? How? Clearly, she doesn't care about the misery and pain she has caused millions of people. She has taken so much from us. Will she do it again? Now we live in constant fear. I hate that fucking bitch. I hope someone shoots her," Claudia said.

"Not sure that can happen," Sinclair said with a shaky voice. "I mean no one touches guns now, and we don't know if she did it. Or has there been something new I missed?"

"I don't know," Claudia said, "but if it was up to me, she would be in prison being tortured until she spoke. Waterboarded or whatever they do. They did it to people for 9-11, and this is a million times worse."

Kate felt her body tremble.

Does everyone hate me? Think I'm responsible?

"Anyway, sorry to digress. I will do some research and let you know if I find anything. Are you heading back to D.C.? I wish I could invite you to stay; under normal circumstances, I would love the company. But I can't. I have a hard time sleeping, and I don't want the virus," Claudia said.

"We understand. We're heading back to D.C., so we should hit the road. Even with the light traffic, it will take a few hours to get back," Sinclair said as he stood up.

Kate cleaned up the snacks as Sinclair walked Claudia to her car. Neither Claudia nor Kate said goodbye, which was fine by Kate. She wanted to run to Sinclair's car and drive away fast. Claudia's vengeful words terrified Kate; she was no longer afraid of only Rex and his violence.

FIVE

Forty-Eight Days After the Shooting

They rode in silence. Kate's hands were trembling. She was still wearing her mask and sunglasses, feeling safer in her disguise.

After some time passed, Sinclair spoke. "I think Claudia is just being reactive. She is an intelligent and loving person and will realize you had nothing to do with the mass shooting, Kate."

Kate just stared out the window for several minutes. *What was I supposed to do? Explain to Claudia that I didn't cause the shooting? That it was actually caused by a pissed-off extraterrestrial who asked me to carry a message to our leaders in order to prevent more violence? That just being a messenger is the extent of my involvement? Yeah, right!*

"More than anything, I hate being called a liar. I hate that anyone would think I was involved with bringing so much pain into the world. I hate that Space Force put my picture out into the media and blamed me for this tragedy. They are the liars! NASA, Space Force, DOD, corporations. They caused the pollution, the dangerous, deadly garbage, not me. I am being blamed. Rex caused the mass shooting, the mass suicide. All those millions of people shot themselves with their own guns. We all know the stats now; almost 40,000 Americans die by guns every year, more than 100 a day, with the majority being suicide. But I am responsible for the mass suicide? Me? A person that loathes guns and violence! Live by the gun, die by the gun. And let's be more specific, live by YOUR gun, die by YOUR gun!" Kate said, almost shouting.

Kate paused and took a few long breaths, holding them for five seconds and releasing them slowly. She was not finished ranting. "And if an intelligent, well-educated, and loving person is willing to think the worst of me from some bullshit on TV with no facts or evidence of any kind, what will the moronic, uneducated haters think of me? They'll definitely blame me. How about taking some personal responsibility? I had to sit there and take her accusations and say nothing. Just like in Colorado. Well, I am going to be damn sure the truth is out there to counter the lies." Kate couldn't help but feel a sense of déjà vu. Just like no one believed her when she tried to inform them of a potential school shooting, the government was refusing to believe her warnings about Rex and the pollution.

Tears of frustration began to pour as she pulled out her phone. Sinclair kept glancing at her, but he did not say a word. He listened as he drove until he realized she was making a call.

"Kate, before you make that call, may I make a suggestion?" Sinclair asked. "You are rightly upset, and I'm infuriated for you. But I don't think we should head back to D.C. yet. You'll be followed and hounded by the press. Sure, the police might provide some protection, but I fear some cops might feel like Claudia does. Police officers, just like all people, can be blinded by fear and rage and behave irrationally. Remember, they lost so many on July 14. Even without guns, they can hurt and kill people. I say this to you as you ride along a highway in the south in a vehicle driven by a Black man," Sinclair added to emphasize his point.

Kate squeezed his arm, acknowledging that she understood him; being judged unfairly and set up to look terrible by the media was not a new thing to Black men.

"People are being irrational because they are afraid and in pain. We need to stick to our plan. We need to find out what caused that collision, the huge explosion in space last year, and why. We need to find out if it was Rex. Once we understand the explosion, I think we will better understand Rex and may be able to slow him down. Hopefully, prevent more violence and save lives," Sinclair said.

Kate nodded. She still had tears streaming down her face. Anger made her cry, and she was still angry.

"Fine. We won't go back," Kate said.

She thought of her boyfriend, Kyle. Sweet, supportive, handsome Kyle, who had no clue what was going on. He risked his life this morning, leading the angry mob away so Kate could safely escape with Sinclair.

"What do you suggest we do?"

"We drive to Texas. Talk to more of Yvette's colleagues and associates. Gather information. Maybe go to California. I have Yvette's computers with me. Get the last encryption cracked and figure out what happened. We can't waste time because we don't know what Rex will do next. What do you think?" Sinclair asked, looking at Kate and not the road.

"Okay. That sounds good. At least we are taking action instead of sitting around hoping someone else will fix the problem. I hate feeling like a useless victim of Space Force and NASA and Rex. Let's go to Texas," Kate said, "but I need to do something now in case we die in a car accident or Rex follows through on his threat."

Kate punched a contact number on her phone. "Hi, mom! How are you?" she said when Jackie answered.

"Okay. I'm okay, but what is happening to you, Kate? I see you on the news as a person of interest in the mass suicide. I'm so worried about you. What is going on?" Jackie asked.

She was speaking very loudly. Kate hadn't heard her mom so upset since Colorado.

"Where are you?" Kate asked, not answering her mom's questions. "Are you still looking after those kids, Leia, Jake, and Katniss? I really love those ridiculous names," Kate added, still in awe that her mom was helping orphans from July 14[th.]

Sinclair gave her a quizzical look.

"Actually, I borrowed a friend's minivan; we are loading it up and soon heading to Tennessee to take the kids to their great-aunt's house. It took a while to locate relatives who are in a position to take the kids. Big gun-loving family. It's so incredibly sad. I booked an alleged COVID-safe Airbnb along the way to break up the drive so the kids don't go nuts. I plan to stay in Knoxville for a few days to make sure everything is okay. I have grown very protective of these little orphans. In fact, why don't you come and meet me? Get out of D.C.; come on a road trip with me. What do you think?" Kate's mom asked. "I am very worried about you, baby."

Under any other circumstances, Kate would love to take a leisurely road trip with her mom.

"I'm so glad you're leaving Florida for a few days. I was going to suggest it, in case the media tracked you down. Best news I have heard in days!" Kate said, relieved. "And it's not just the media being obnoxious. There are people who believe I had something to do with the shooting, and they are angry. Irrational, angry people are very scary. I am really happy you are heading out of town. When do you leave?"

"As soon as I get the kids in the car. We are packed up and snacked up and almost ready to roll. The kiddos are right here. Say hi to Kate. She needs some good energy," Kate's mom said loudly so the kids could hear.

"Hi Kate!" their childish voices shouted and squealed.

"Thanks, Mom, I did need that. Hello and hugs to them! Listen, I am going to make a recording of what's been happening and send it to you. Don't listen until they're asleep because it's a weird and upsetting story. I need you to save the recording. I just need someone I trust and love to know the whole story. The whole truth. Okay? Like before," Kate gulped. "You were the only one who believed me in Colorado. Drive safely. Slow and steady, Mom. I will call you tomorrow," Kate said, trying to end the call. She did not want to delay her mom's departure.

"Hold on. Are you in danger? Like of being arrested? Tell me the story now, Kate. This seems so similar to Colorado. Almost as bad as Colorado! How is that? Tell me what's going on," Kate's mom implored.

Damn. Now I've scared her. Not my intent.

"I'm totally fine. I promise. It's too long to get into now. Yes, it's eerily similar to Colorado in a way, but not exactly bad." *More like terrifying, horrific, and deadly.* "I'm on a road trip with a friend," Kate said, wincing as she tried not to lie.

"Kyle?" Jackie asked.

"No, Kyle's holding down the fort," Kate said, feeling a twinge of guilt. "I'll call you tomorrow, Mom. Maybe we can get our paths to cross. I love you and I will talk to you tomorrow," Kate said, ending the call and wiping away tears.

"You are right, Sinclair. The world is full of assholes, but it's also full of innocents who don't deserve any of this. We must do all we can, and as quickly as we can, to prevent more violence," Kate said as she looked out the window, eyes warily scanning the landscape.

"What happened in Colorado?" Sinclair asked.

SIX

Forty-Eight Days After the Shooting

"**C**olorado was a long time ago, and it's not relevant," Kate replied.

Kate looked out across the four-lane, mostly empty highway. Green pastures, some with cows, flew by. They passed an occasional billboard with smiling unmasked faces, reminding her of the world before the pandemic and the shooting.

"I'm curious, and if you don't mind sharing, I would like to know," Sinclair said.

Kate took an audible deep breath before replying, "Okay, Colorado. I was born in Colorado and lived in the burbs outside Denver. One day when I was in middle school, in seventh grade, I was walking…"

Kate's story was interrupted when the Tesla Roadster fell out of the sky several hundred feet to the right of the highway.

SEVEN

Forty-Eight Days After the Shooting

"It's a sign or warning from Rex," Kate repeated, her voice shaking with fear.

Sinclair took pictures with his phone.

"We're in danger. The world is in danger. We better go, Sinclair. If I'm seen anywhere near this thing, I am done," Kate said over her shoulder as she pulled him, rushing back to his car. "They'll blame me."

Hearts pounding, they climbed back into the car.

Sinclair peeled back onto the road, tires squealing as they drove away.

"That car belongs to another space-loving billionaire, not Yvette's friend, Jack," Sinclair said excitedly.

The impact of what they just saw—and barely dodged—was sinking in.

Am I a magnet for disaster?

"I know. I remember when it was launched, like late 2017 or maybe 2018. I did not think about it at first, because, you know, why would it come back to

Earth right now? What are the chances that it nearly crash-lands on us?" Kate asked, talking quickly since she was nervous. "Sinclair, it doesn't make sense. It won't make sense to those other people that saw it fall and are back there taking pictures. It won't make sense to NASA. How could it survive re-entry? I'm not an astrophysicist, and even I know it's too small to remain intact. It'll make no sense to anyone except those that know about Rex. It could have hit us. It could have landed on us or the road. This a warning!"

"Jesus," Sinclair said, "you're right. Sorry, I just had to see it up close to believe it."

"I wonder if there were others," Kate said, looking at her phone and realizing there was no internet connection. She clicked on the radio, scrolling for news.

"This is a breaking news story. There are multiple reports that an object has crashed on the National Mall in Washington, D.C.," said an NPR correspondent. "We are waiting for confirmation on what it is and whether anyone was hurt in the incident. D.C. police and Secret Service are rushing to the object now. We hope for an update soon and will bring it to you live."

Kate and Sinclair rode in silence, listening to the story as it unfolded.

The reporter continued, "I just got confirmation that the objects which landed on the National Mall in Washington appear to be satellites. They fell out of the sky and landed on the grassy area near the Washington Monument. We are working to determine the origin of the satellites and the reason for the fall. It appears from preliminary video footage that at least one person was struck by the objects, a runner near the Mall. If it weren't for the pandemic canceling tourists' summer plans, the human toll could have been much, much worse."

"That is so sad. That runner was enjoying a healthy, beautiful run, and bam, dead," Kate said to the radio. "It's more violence."

Sinclair pulled off the highway, bringing Kate's focus back to look around at her surroundings.

"Why are we getting off?" Kate asked.

"We need gas, food, internet, and a TV," Sinclair replied, pulling into an empty motel parking lot.

"It looks closed," Kate said.

"Highway billboard said this place was open for business and taking precautions against COVID," Sinclair replied.

Sinclair put on his mask, Kate put on her disguise, and they walked into the reception area. The television in the lobby was showing a movie, not the news. Sinclair rang the bell, and they waited.

"Hi, folks, how are you?" a teenager asked, coming from the office behind the desk.

"Okay," Sinclair replied. "You're open for guests, right?"

"I guess. You are the first people in a few days," the kid replied.

"Do you have good, reliable internet in the rooms?" Sinclair asked.

"Yes, of course. We're a national chain," the teenager replied.

"Okay, two rooms, next door to each other," Sinclair said.

They did some paperwork, and the kid walked them to the rooms. On the way, he stopped, entered a closet, and pulled out a cart. Suddenly, a woman appeared, walking toward them from the other direction.

"Please wait out here as we take proper COVID precautions for the rooms," the kid said as he unlocked one room. He opened the curtains and windows and proceeded to clean every surface with a strong-smelling disinfectant. The woman did the same in the other room.

Kate and Sinclair were leaning on Sinclair's car watching the procedure.

"This seems excessive. Didn't he just say they haven't had guests in days?" Sinclair asked Kate impatiently. "I really want to know what is going on. We have no idea how many objects fell out of the sky. Wonder if the local news is covering the car?"

"If your stay is acceptable and you write a review, please add that you witnessed this high-caliber cleaning and knew your room was properly sterilized," the kid called loudly through the window to be heard. "We would appreciate it."

"Of course. We appreciate the attention to detail," Kate said loudly so the woman cleaning the other room could hear it as well.

"Where can we get something to eat around here?" Sinclair asked as the kid walked out and returned the cleaning products to the cart.

"Nowhere, really. It's Monday and nothing is open. Most of our traffic comes from people taking a break while traveling elsewhere, but the pandemic brought that to a screeching halt. Then the shooting wiped out half the town. Maybe more. Whole families are dead. The grocery store is only open Thursday through Sunday because there are so few staff to work the shifts. And so few shoppers. It was a real bloodbath," the kid added.

"Sorry to hear that. That is terrible. What about the gas station?" Sinclair asked, seeming slightly alarmed.

"Yes, the gas station is open. Every day until midnight," the kid replied.

"Okay. That's good. At least we can get gas and snacks," Sinclair said to Kate.

"There's a sandwich shop in the gas station," the woman said as she came out of the room. "I'll call my grandmother. She can meet you there and make some sandwiches. She lives across the highway. I will let you know when she will be there."

"Wow, thanks, that is so helpful," Kate said as her stomach let out a long wail.

Have I had any food today?

Sinclair and Kate entered the same motel room. Sinclair plugged in his computer and Kate turned on the TV. The shot was of smoldering debris on the

Mall and firefighters milling about. It seemed they had put the flames out and were trying to determine what happened.

A reporter appeared in front of the shot of the debris and said, "The fires have been put out and we now know two satellites fell out of the sky and crashed onto the National Mall, just feet away from the Washington Monument, only several hundred feet away from the White House. We have learned similar satellite crashes occurred in Moscow and Beijing. No one knows why the satellites malfunctioned. No one knows how they made it back to Earth without disintegrating. We are also trying to determine how many people were killed or injured from the impacts."

"Jesus Christ," Sinclair said quietly, staring at the TV.

They both jumped when the room phone rang.

"Hello?" Kate answered it.

"Hi, my grandmother is at the shop. You should go now. She can't wait around," the woman from earlier said into the phone.

"Okay. Sure. Yes. Thanks," Kate said before hanging up.

She turned off the TV, and they got in the car and drove to the gas station. They were both quiet. They both looked up at the sky multiple times on the short drive. Kate glanced over her shoulder through the back window as well, looking for violence.

The other satellites fell in significant places. The Tesla practically fell on us. What is Rex saying?

When they arrived, Sinclair pumped gas and Kate went for sandwiches and supplies. She said hello to the person at the counter, seeming to be the only customer in the store. She found the sandwich shop in the back by following kids' giggling voices. She heard children laughing and playing behind the counter.

"What can I get you?" a very old woman asked.

Kate assumed that she was the grandmother and realized the children were probably the reason she could not wait around. Kate watched the kids chase one another and wondered what happened to their parents. *Did some of them shoot themselves in front of these children?*

Kate ordered four vegan sandwiches, basically salad on wheat bread, figuring dinner and breakfast, and left a big tip, making the woman's effort to come in worth it.

She found a well-stocked personal hygiene area and picked up travel-sized floss, moisturizer, sunblock, toothpaste, Advil, and even a decent hairbrush. She also picked up a couple of phone chargers, a gallon of drinking water, and some other necessities.

She was making trips back and forth to the counter as she gathered more things, leaving them next to the sandwiches.

"Okay, I think that is it," she said to the man behind the counter. "Oh shoot, I don't have any money." Kate pulled out the last bill from the cash Sinclair gave her earlier. It was a five-dollar bill, and Kate figured she probably had forty dollars' worth of stuff on the counter.

"But I do," Sinclair said, coming up behind Kate and startling her. She was surprised she did not hear him. The store had been so quiet as she shopped, eerily quiet. Even the kids must have left.

"We scored big," Kate said, nodding at the loot on the counter, including the large bag of sandwiches.

"That is not a score; those are necessities. These are scores," Sinclair said, holding up a bottle of Pinot Noir in one hand and a pint of non-dairy ice cream in the other. "I hope the wine is not too terrible. It's very cheap."

"No, not terrible. That was my favorite brand of wine when I was in college," Kate said, almost laughing. She felt a little drunk already, unsteady and light-headed, even though she had not had a sip. She blamed it on the low blood sugar and lingering adrenalin.

They drove back to the motel in silence, except for Kate's stomach wailing in hunger.

Back in the room, Kate plugged in her phone to charge and quickly scarfed down a sandwich while staring at the TV. Sinclair ate slower, flipping channels. There did not seem to be any new information since they returned from the gas station. Sinclair opened the wine and handed Kate a plastic cup. Kate ripped open the ice cream.

"It used to be that wine and ice cream could make anything better. Like magic. Well, until deadly viruses, mass shootings, cars falling out of the sky, and Rex ruined it," Kate said.

She put the ice cream down and stretched out on one of the beds.

"If I doze off, wake me up when they know something. Anything. Of course, what will they know?

Right? We know more than anyone. More than anyone in the entire world," Kate mumbled as her eyes closed, and she fell asleep.

Sinclair was sitting at the little table working on his computer and watching the TV.

"Good night, Kate," he whispered as Kate fell asleep.

EIGHT

Forty-Nine Days After
the Shooting

K ate jerked awake, terrified, trying to understand where she was. Then the whole day came tumbling down on her conscience, and she closed her eyes tightly, almost in pain. She remembered running from a mob, driving to Virginia where a woman called her a fucking bitch and wished her dead, and an electric car falling out of the sky.

Did all of this happen in just one day?

She knew she was not going to fall back asleep.

As her eyes adjusted to the darkness, she realized she was fully dressed, minus shoes, under the blankets. She looked over at the other bed and was surprised to see Sinclair's form on it. She assumed he would have gone to the other room.

She quietly got up, put her shoes on, and grabbed the bag of gas station hygiene products. As she crept past Sinclair, she saw that he was lying on his stomach, asleep across the bed, the bedspread not turned down.

He had one shoe on. Kate figured he probably intended to go to the other room but, like her, crashed hard.

As she quietly opened the door, she heard him snore softly and was happy she did not wake him.

Kate went to the other room, brushed her teeth, washed her face, and plopped on the bed, figuring she would scroll through social media and watch the news, but she had had enough for one day. She did not need or want more information. She needed to take a minute and relay information. She walked out of the room and slowly paced the motel parking lot under the stars and half-moon. It was very quiet at almost 2:00 a.m. She hit record on her phone and made a video.

"Hi, Mom. Like I said I would, I am making you a video so someone I know and trust and love knows the truth. It's around 2:00 a.m. I am somewhere in Virginia at a motel with a neighbor who has become a good friend; his name is Sinclair Jones. It's dark because I am walking around the parking lot. I can't sleep.

Anyway, I'll start at the beginning.

As you know, I was running in Rock Creek Park on the day of the mass shooting. A few days later, I was running in the same location and was somehow snatched, flown super-fast through the air, and placed in a white room with an avatar of some type that shifted forms. He mostly took the form of Barack Obama that time. He warned me to tell the leaders at Space Force that more violence was coming. After talking to me, I was placed back at the trail where I was taken from. At the time, I didn't think it was real; I decided that I must have hallucinated because I was overheated from the weather and stressed from the shooting and pandemic.

Several days later, it happened again. This time the avatar turned into a huge, orange cat that reminded me of a former foster cat, Rex. The avatar became 'Rex' to me. Same warning, but this time I was told to relay the message or more violence would come within five days.

Even though I questioned my sanity, I told my boss at Space Force and my neighbor, Sinclair, who works at NASA, what happened. Although, I changed the story to say that Rex was a crazy guy harassing me with the warning in the park, leaving out the snatching, white room, Obama, and cat. I didn't want anyone to think I was crazy. I hoped that if I did what I was told, all would be well, and Rex would leave me alone. But you and I both know it is easier to blame the messenger, so Space Force and others focused their attention on me. I was followed and interviewed.

Rex has snatched me up a couple more times, with the warnings becoming more specific and dire. I was told to tell the leaders at Space Force and NASA to clean up the dangerous pollution or there would be more violence. I gave this information to Space Force leadership. I gave them all the information, including about Rex. They threw me under the bus and leaked to the public that I was a person of interest, allowing the world to believe that I was the mastermind behind the shooting or covering for someone."

Kate paused and took a few deep breaths.

"So, now Sinclair, who is an astrophysicist at NASA, and I are out trying to learn about a collision in space last year which we think somehow set off Rex. I pleaded with Space Force to clean up the dangerous pollution, but they weren't receptive; they said it was too hard and too expensive and found it easier to blame me. Sinclair and I are just hoping to find out what happened in space and maybe find a way to work with Rex; at the very least, we hope to buy some time or find a way to stop additional violence."

Kate thought she heard a noise coming from the highway. She whipped around, staring into the darkness, her heart pounding. After hearing only crickets and normal night sounds, she continued.

"That is everything in a nutshell. That is why I can't meet you on your drive to Tennessee. I need you to keep all this information to yourself. With satellites and a car falling out of space, I am not sure what will happen to me. Rex is angry. Rex is sending warnings. We have to find a way to stop him before you and Kyle and baby Katniss and so many other innocent people are hurt or killed."

Kate continued to walk in circles in the mostly empty parking lot, occasionally pausing to listen for any strange sounds.

"I know that this is a lot to take in. Please know that I love you, and we can discuss this, and more, soon. I feel better than I have in days just telling you this. Thanks, Mom! I love you! Goodbye for now!"

Kate stopped the recording and played it back for herself, checking to see if she sounded too crazy.

I think it sounds okay. Fitting for the situation, but not too crazy.

She walked closer to the rooms and hit send. Her mom would have it when she woke up.

Kate jumped a foot in the air when Sinclair opened the door and whispered loudly, "Kate, is that you? Who are you talking to? Are you okay?"

"Ah, yes, you startled me! Sorry. I did not mean to wake you," Kate said.

"No, you did not wake me. I just woke up and figured you went next door, but then I heard talking and got worried. Are you okay? Who are you talking to?" Sinclair asked again.

"Myself. And my mom. I made a video on my phone. All is well, all things considered. I think we should try to get more sleep. It's really late, or really early. I feel like I could sleep some more. What about you?" Kate asked.

"Yes, yes, I think so. Okay. Goodnight, Kate," Sinclair said, closing the motel room door.

Kate walked into the other room and headed straight for the bed. Her last thought before she fell asleep was that moms, like wine and ice cream, made everything okay.

Or used to.

NINE

Forty-Nine Days After the Shooting

Kate was tossing and turning from another nightmare. Her mom was driving down a highway, singing a pop song with the kids when a red electric car crashed on the roof. Other cars ran into the crash, and there were so many explosions, like a terrible action movie.

Kate jerked awake.

She quickly jumped up, showered, and used her limited bathroom products to prepare for the day. She tidied the room, collected her few belongings, and headed next door. She had planned to knock, but Sinclair had the curtains open, and she could see him sitting at the table, working on his computer.

"Good morning, Sinclair. How did you sleep?" Kate asked as she entered the room.

"Okay, considering. I've been mapping out our drive to Texas. It's a 24-hour straight shot, so I figure three days for us if we drive eight hours a day. Arrive

Thursday night, if it goes smoothly. I will schedule some meetings with Yvette's contacts for Friday. We can stop in a city tonight, hit a Target or something, and get more supplies. We need clothes. What do you think?" Sinclair asked.

Kate nodded in agreement to Sinclair's plan as she opened the minifridge, intending to grab the last sandwich. She saw the wrappings of one next to Sinclair, realizing he had already had breakfast. Instead, she picked up the ice cream. She stuck it in the microwave for a few seconds and then plopped on the bed with it.

"This won't last in the car. Can't have melting ice cream all over," she explained to Sinclair as she dove into what was left in the pint. "And we may die soon, so let's live a little. Ice cream for breakfast until the end." Kate clicked on the TV. "Anything new? More satellites or cars from space? More violence?"

"No. So far everyone seems focused on the satellites. As of an hour ago, they were just repeating what we knew last night and speculating. Many, many experts speculating on why the objects fell from space. All of them are wrong, of course. Space Force and NASA statements were vague and meaningless. I think they're still trying to figure out what to say. Trying to get their stories straight. They must be struggling with how much to tell their staff. The experts in the agencies will know this cannot happen. The objects are too small and should have disintegrated," Sinclair said, looking at his computer.

"Oh no, this looks new," Kate said as the anchor turned it over to a local correspondent in southern Virginia.

"Yesterday, around the same time the satellites landed in Washington, D.C., we had some local excitement as a car seemed to have come out of nowhere and crashed into a field along highway 12. Local investigators spent the night trying to figure out where it came from and why. They were speaking to a handful of witnesses who saw the car crash in the field and are looking for more witnesses. Earlier this morning, investigators from NASA and Space Force arrived. We are all eager to hear if this car, like the satellites, fell from space. Luckily, there were no injuries," the correspondent finished and turned it back to the national anchor.

"They don't seem to know anything real yet about the car. Or are not saying. But people will figure it out soon. Space reporters, analysts, and fans are going to figure out whose electric vehicle it is and where it came from," Kate summarized. "I bet it's on Twitter already."

A loud bang on the door made both of them jump.

"Jesus, who's there?" Sinclair shouted as he got up to see out the window.

"It's me, from reception," the kid said, looking in the window.

"I realized we didn't put coffee in the rooms yesterday. There is a fresh pot in the reception area, or you can use these," he said, holding up little packets of coffee for the room coffeemaker.

As Sinclair opened the door to get the coffee, the kid added, "Check out is 11:00 a.m., but feel free to check out later. Since you're the only guests, we can be flexible."

"Okay, thanks," Sinclair said, taking the coffee and turning to close the door.

"What time do you plan to check out? I want to be sure to be at the desk," he added.

Sinclair opened the door wide, so the kid could clearly see in the room.

Kate glanced away, covering her face with her hands like a mask so the kid could not see her face.

"We don't have any incidentals or costs and have paid, so we will just leave when we are ready. Thank you for your hospitality," Sinclair said and shut the door.

"That was odd. He seems very nosey," Kate said. "You did not have to show him the room. We paid. He said we could check out late. It's none of his business what we are doing in here."

"I was showing him the room was fine. We are fine. I think it's a Black man thing in the south. I just don't want any trouble. Remove ridiculous speculation," Sinclair said as he made coffee.

"Wow," Kate said, "I knew things were different for Black and White Americans, but I had not thought of that. Sorry."

"What do you think of the plan? The drive to Texas?" Sinclair asked, changing the subject.

"I think it's a good plan. Taking action. Trying to figure out how to stop the violence and satisfy Rex's demands. We can take turns driving," Kate said, finishing off the ice cream and heading to the fridge for the sandwich.

Kate focused on watching the news as she ate.

"Interesting though that the mass shooting is not the lead story; I bet that's the first time since July 14. And look, the pandemic death clock is just in a little box in the corner like when they advertise for one TV show during another. Not even a scroll. People have so many reasons to be scared, terrified," Kate mumbled as Sinclair typed.

"Did that kid seem oddly calm? He didn't say a word about the car falling from space and it was what, 20 miles away from here? He must have heard about it by now, and it's not like anything else is happening in this Podunk town. He was nosey about us, but no gossip about the car," Kate said louder, putting down what was left of her sandwich.

She suddenly felt a chill run down her spine.

"I think we need to leave soon, Sinclair," Kate said, getting up off the bed.

What if his curiosity wasn't just about a Black man traveling with a White woman? What if he recognized me?

Just before 9:00 a.m., they drove quickly out of the motel parking lot. The kid rushed out of the reception office and watched them drive away. He did not smile or wave.

TEN

Forty-Nine Days After
the Shooting

As they drove away, Yvette's phone rang. Kate answered, pressed speaker, and held it close for Sinclair to speak.

"Hello, this is Sinclair," he said.

"Sinclair, it's Jack. Dude, what in the hell is going on?" he demanded impatiently.

"Hi Jack, about what in particular? Are you wondering about the satellites falling out of space and landing on Earth?" Sinclair asked calmly like he had expected this call.

"Well, yes, that of course, and you know whose car. Have you heard about that? Supposedly the car was on its way to Mars. Ha! He must be pretty ticked off that it's back!" Jack said with a loud laugh.

I wonder if this is normal for competing space billionaires to not say each other's names. It seems juvenile, very consistent with their personalities.

"Yes. I heard. It's unreal. You know it's not possible; it defies gravity and physics," Sinclair responded.

"Right. Of course. Totally impossible. Where are you right now?" Jack asked.

"I'm on a road trip with a friend looking into Yvette's research, as we discussed on Sunday. It's only been a day, so I haven't found out much yet. But I am working on it," Sinclair said.

"I think as you look into what caused the colossal collision last year, you should also look into what caused the satellites and car to come crashing down yesterday. I'll pay you really well for whatever you find out," Jack said.

"Sure, Jack, but I'm not sure the two are related. I plan to look into everything that I can," Sinclair said, raising his eyebrows at Kate. "Was one of the satellites yours? Or was your equipment damaged?"

"None of my stuff came down; that I know for sure. But it's all related. Something strange is happening. Dude, NASA knows more than it's revealing," Jack said.

"Why do you say that, Jack?" Sinclair asked.

"Because when I got home this morning and parked my car, one of my other cars, a gorgeous new Tesla, was smashed into the ground. Smashed. Guess what fell on it, Sinclair? Take a wild guess," Jack said.

"I have no idea," Sinclair said, shrugging.

"A NASA tool bag; one of the thirty-pound tool bags for Space Station repairs with their logo printed all over it. They cost at least $100K, and it was somewhat intact, unlike my car which is not intact, not at all," Jack said in an excited and agitated voice. "Find out what the hell is happening, Sinclair. Find out before one of my satellites or ships comes down or needs to go up. Find out before something lands on my house or launch pads or offices or my fucking head. Where are you? Did you say on a road trip? To where exactly?"

"I thought the tool bag disintegrated a decade ago. It entered our atmosphere and poof, gone," Sinclair said. "Oh, and Texas. We are heading to Texas."

"Well, I guess they lost another one and didn't tell us," Jack responded, "because it flattened my car. Too much of a coincidence that satellites and like that douchebag's roadster to Mars came hurtling down from space. Then this NASA tool bag fell out of a plane? And just happened to land on my car?" Jack asked, sounding very upset.

"Jack, I am going to look into it. So will NASA, Space Force, and probably DOD as well. This is a big deal because national security is involved. Just stay calm and safe," Sinclair said.

"When will you get to Texas?" Jack asked.

"Friday if all goes well. We should be in Houston on Friday. We plan to go straight to Yvette's office at Johnson," Sinclair explained.

"Cool, I'll meet you there. We should also look into that Space Force woman, Kate Stellute; she definitely knows something. Find out everything you can about her," Jack said as he hung up.

ELEVEN

Forty-Nine Days After the Shooting

"**W**hat the heck, Sinclair? A NASA tool bag smashed his car? Do you know what this means? Rex is definitely sending a message. He is tossing our space garbage back at us. Hopefully, Space Force and NASA are taking this seriously. They need to start a clean-up project now," Kate said, putting the pieces together in her head. "And Jack's last words were ominous. Do we really want to meet him in Texas? Do you trust him?"

Kate's phone exploded with texts from her mom.

[MOM: Saw you sent a video but with the chaos of getting 3 kids up and out, I didn't have time to watch it yet. We hit the road really early. They slept in the car a long time, thank God, and just now needed a bathroom break.]

[MOM: I will try to watch at lunch break.]

[MOM: Are you okay?]

[MOM: I need to change Katniss.]

[MOM: Leia and Jake are so helpful. It's adorable.]

[MOM: But are you okay?????]

Kate texted back:

[KATE: Yes. Mom. I am totally fine. Driving with Sinclair.]

[KATE: Don't worry about the video. Watch it tonight when kids are asleep. Seriously – I am good.]

[KATE: Just drive safe.]

[KATE: I will call you tonight.]

[KATE: I love you!]

Kate's mom texted back:

[MOM: I love you too!!! Stay safe!]

[MOM: Hugs to Sinclair. Can't wait to meet him!]

"My mom is so sweet. She texted hugs to you, and she can't wait to meet you," Kate told Sinclair.

"Your mom is an angel. Must be hard. That's a long drive with two little kids and a toddler," Sinclair responded.

"Seriously, I can't even imagine it. Okay. Let's focus. Who knows where we are?" Kate said, jumping topics.

"Everyone. Everyone who wants to," Sinclair said. "They can track our phones, and I have been using my credit card. Anyone that wants to know where we are, knows. That is a fact."

"So, they know we were near the electric car last night, they know what motel we stayed in, and they know we are heading to Texas. They probably also know we talked to Jack." Kate wanted clarity on the situation.

"Yep. Safe to assume that is all correct. They may have talked to the kid at reception. Maybe that was why he was being nosy," Sinclair said. "Interesting that they are just letting us go. Letting us do our thing. I mean, they could pick us up right now."

Sinclair glanced up at the sky as Kate looked over her shoulder.

"The traffic is so light. I feel like we are in some horror zombie movie, and we should get off the highway," Kate said. "I guess they are all doing the same thing, watching us. Rex is watching us to see what we do, and where we go. Rex wants to know what Space Force or NASA or the government will do to us and the dangerous pollution. And Space Force, NASA, and the government are watching us to see if we will lead them to Rex."

Kate's phone rang and they both jumped.

"It's Kyle. I better answer. He must be worried," Kate said to Sinclair.

"Hi, babe! How are you?" Kate said as she picked up.

"I'm okay, Kate. How are you? *Where* are you?" Kyle asked.

Shoot. He sounds mad.

Their last conversation was terrible; she'd lied to him for the first time in their relationship. Now she'd have to lie again. *Or do I? If NASA and the government know where I am, can't I tell him the truth?*

"New York was a bust. Heading south now. Sinclair has another lead we want to check out. Where are you?" Kate asked, trying to say as little as possible.

"Home, of course. We're still in a pandemic. I hope you are being really careful, Kate. Remember how much we value our sense of smell. Even if we are statistically safer than most, we don't even want to get it, right? Are you being careful out there?" Kyle asked, sounding sincerely concerned.

"Yes, we are being super careful. I promise," Kate replied. "What is happening there? What time did you get home?"

"The last we spoke; I was outside the police station drinking coffee. Soon after, two young cops took me home. Lady cops. They are so young. They explained they are right out of the academy. They graduated a few weeks after the mass shooting. They did not have guns on July 14. So, these baby cops drove me home and they had street closure barricades that read "police action—no thru traffic" and we put them up on both ends of the block. I helped. They chased what was left of the mob and reporters back beyond the barricades. They were awesome though, these badass baby cops," Kyle said. He was enjoying telling the story; Kate could hear in his voice that he was smiling.

"Wow, that's cool Kyle. I am so happy they made it safe," Kate replied.

"That was around 3:00 p.m. The cops stayed in their car on the block, just watching. Things were quiet. Several neighbors came over and were like "what the heck is going on?" And so I told them the story. How Rex harassed you in the park and people were confused and thought you knew something about the shooting, but it was just this big misunderstanding. I said the media ran with the garbage because that's what the media does. They love a big story, and anything about the shooting is a big story. We all agreed we felt safer with the police there and hoped they would stay all night. Eventually, everyone left, the neighbors and media, and things were calm … for a few hours anyway," Kyle said and then paused.

Kate did not say a word as she felt her heart start to beat faster.

"It seems some satellites crashed down on the Mall, and reporters and crowds came back and started gathering near the barricades. It was getting louder and more unruly, kind of like on Monday morning. Neighbors started calling. One cop was at each barricade. It was getting stressful. The news kept saying the incident might be tied to the mass shooting. Some in the media, mostly on Twitter, were saying maybe Kate Stellute, the person of interest, knew what was happening. By eleven, it was getting out of control, so I took care of it," Kyle said.

Yes, they blame me. Just as we feared.

"How did you take care of it, babe?" Kate asked. Sinclair could hear the conversation; Kyle was talking loudly.

"I went out to the barricade with the biggest crowd and took your bullhorn with me, the one I bought you for Christmas last year. I went out there and said into the bullhorn, 'I'm Kyle, Kate's boyfriend. We live together. Kate is not here. She went on a trip with a friend. You can shout all you want. You can knock down the barricades. You can throw things in our window. You can do whatever you want, but it won't matter because you can't talk to Kate because she is not here.' Then one of the cool, baby cops, Amanda, took the bullhorn and added that if anyone did any of those things I had just said, they could be arrested," Kyle said.

Kate loved him so much. "Oh my god Kyle, that was so risky and dangerous. What happened next?"

"Amanda told me to go inside. She said I wasn't being helpful. The crowd was shouting questions at me and yelling that I was harboring a killer. They screamed that you had killed millions. Crazy shit like that. So, I went into the house, thinking Amanda was right. I had not helped anything. But then like an hour later, almost everyone left. I guess it sank in that you were not here so there was no point in staying all night. Although a few did; some were sleeping on the ground in the morning, and there were three vans parked nearby that never left. I think they were reporters watching the street to see if you came home. It turns out that I was helpful in the end. Amanda even acknowledged it. I let the cops use the bathroom and WIFI and offered them drinks throughout the night. I knew I wasn't going to be able to sleep," Kyle continued his story. "I finally crashed around 4:00 a.m. and slept until just an hour ago. Aside from the crazy people sleeping on the street and those in the vans, it's pretty quiet. Where are you exactly, Kate?" Kyle asked.

Sinclair and Kate looked at each other; they both knew they could not trust Kyle. He would talk thinking he was being helpful. Sure, Space Force and the government knew where they were, but Kyle could accidentally tip off the press and a mob.

"We're heading to Pennsylvania. Sinclair has another lead. Another brilliant space scientist that kind of cracked up. He might be under too much stress. He might be Rex," Kate winced as she said it.

This was straight-up lying to her boyfriend, her best friend in the world, and it hurt. "Or he may know where Rex is."

"I thought you said you were heading south?" Kyle asked, sounding suspicious.

"Well, south of New York. We were in New York yesterday. Heading south now," Kate replied.

"Oh, okay. How long will you be gone?" Kyle asked.

"I honestly don't know, babe. If we find him or something that will help the investigation, we will be home soon. But if not, we can't just give up. Right?" Kate asked.

"I guess not," Kyle responded. "What part of Pennsylvania? I know a lot of people there. Maybe I can help?"

"Pittsburgh part of the state, not Philly," Kate crossed her fingers to neuter the lie; she had forgotten Kyle was from Philadelphia. "I think it's my turn to drive. Give Sinclair a break. I'll call you later, okay? Please be careful. Please listen to Amanda. No more heroics, with or without a bullhorn. Okay, Kyle?" Kate asked, trying to lighten the mood.

"Okay, but promise me you'll get a cup of coffee before you get behind that steering wheel. Tell Sinclair driving makes you tired. Engines do something to your brain. I worry when you drive. Tell that to Sinclair now, so I can hear it," he demanded.

"Okay. Sinclair, Kyle says I need a cup of coffee when I drive. We should get some when we switch. Sinclair is nodding in agreement. Okay, Kyle? I'll call you tonight. Stay safe; I love you," Kate said.

"I love you too, Kate. Stay safe and stay awake. I hope you find Rex. Bye for now," Kyle said as he hung up the phone.

Kate put her phone down and began rubbing her eyes.

"So many lies, Sinclair. How will I keep them straight? When I'm home and he is asking a hundred questions, how will I keep it straight?" Kate asked.

"By the time you get home, hopefully, you can tell him the whole truth," Sinclair responded.

"It'll be too late. He'll ask me why I lied in the first place. How can I tell him that I didn't trust his judgment to be quiet? This totally sucks. Right this minute, I really hate Rex." Kate sighed.

"Only right this minute? Let's not forget he killed millions of people, including Yvette," Sinclair said.

Kate looked out the window.

Technically they killed themselves. Live by the gun, die by the gun. The violence, the guns, and the pollution were put into the world by individuals, and it is coming back at them. Karma.

She did not share her thoughts with Sinclair.

"Do you want me to drive?" Kate asked. "If so, I'll need that cup of coffee."

TWELVE

Forty-Nine Days After the Shooting

Sinclair was still driving. Kate was anxious, waiting for the phone to ring with bad news. She found herself checking the skyline every time her thoughts got the best of her.

"Let's check the news," Sinclair suggested, watching Kate get twitchy. "A little NPR. See if the experts are making a statement. Or hear what the conspiracy crowd is claiming. Could be entertaining," Sinclair said.

When he found a clear news station, they could hear the owner of the Tesla Roadster which crashed back to Earth giving his theory about why it happened.

"So, Jack had it shot down somehow. Or Linus. Or the "bleeping" Chinese. Maybe Putin? All a bunch of jealous assholes. Jealous I got it into the asteroid belt. Jealous it was on its way to Mars. They know I control space exploration now. They are all a bunch of douchebags," he ranted at a reporter with his strong, Boston accent.

"If that is the case, why shoot down the satellites? They were not yours. Those that crashed in Washington D.C. were the property of the U.S. government," the brave reporter said.

"I have no f'ing idea, but I will find out soon and sue their asses and destroy their programs," he continued to rant.

"NASA has several pieces of equipment on Mars, as does Russia, and China has equipment on its way. Why target your car? The Tesla was a fun joke, but you have serious missions planned. Are you worried about your other equipment? It's all so curious. Do you have any real leads?" the reporter asked.

"Oh, screw off, you tosser," he replied, and the interview was over.

"He knows nothing about his car. I can hear the raw frustration in his voice. I do wonder how much he knows about you and Rex? Jack seems pretty knowledgeable. He's on the right trail," Sinclair said, turning the radio down.

"That's because of Yvette, and you," Kate replied. "Jack has people on the inside, probably because he's not as much of an asshole as the other space billionaire boys' club members. I am starting to see that the space industry is just the ongoing paternalistic, colonial, White male domination; it's the 'might and wealth makes right' control bullshit that has existed since the beginning of time. I thought space exploration was noble. I thought of it as the quest for knowledge. With each launch, we learned new things about space, materials, technology, and our planet's origin. It was so exciting to me, and I was thrilled to be a part of it. At first, Mars seemed so sexy. Getting there is so dangerous. I wanted to help, even with just my small contract analyst contribution; I wanted to help get humans safely to Mars."

"You, like most people, watch too many movies, Kate," Sinclair said.

"Let's say NASA gets there, or Jack or the Chinese. Then what? What is there? What will we learn? Like everything in this capitalistic, toxic White male world, it is turning so dark and abusive. It's not just education and science for the sake of education and science, it's a race to get there and dominate it. It's just like when America was supposedly discovered by the Europeans. Find any life or resources, steal them, use them, and leave a terrible mess for someone else to clean up, or just never clean it up," Kate sighed and was silent for a few minutes. She looked out the windows, watching rolling hills and green pastures fly past.

"And we are destroying this world with pollution and plastic and climate change and threatening all animals and plants with extinction. Look at this planet. Look at how beautiful it is. We abuse nature and treat the air and water like toilets and garbage cans. We literally shit all over everything. We recklessly extract metals, food, animals, and water in the most wasteful and abusive ways, soothing our minds by thinking we can go live on Mars when this planet is uninhabitable. Do you think it's intentional? Like gaslighting and brainwashing the whole populace? Because even if we get there and make it habitable, not everyone is going. Only the rich and powerful will get to Mars," Kate said, tears of frustration flowing down her face. "We have until 2030 to turn it all around, stop the climate and extinction crisis, or it's game over. And the media runs more stories about space exploration than both crises combined."

Kate felt a wave of self-hatred for her contributions to all of it.

"The thing that kills me, Kate, is how much money is spent on space exploration. Don't get me wrong, I was enamored with it as much as you. More, I spent a decade in school learning everything I could to help the missions, and I've worked for NASA for years. There are still good intentions for space exploration, but it needs to be done in a more sustainable and logical way. You know, when it started in the '50s, probably into the '90s, we thought Earth was too big to destroy; we know better now. You still hear old-timers say, 'The solution to pollution is dilution.' That is not true. Not here or in space," Sinclair said. "We should be spending the billions we do on space to put solar panels on every roof, consume less, pollute less. There is never enough money to help the environment, education, or real criminal justice reform, or to help people get healthcare, but there are billions to get to Mars. We should fix our problems here first, then focus on space."

"And who wants to live on Mars anyway? I have said it before and I will say it again, I don't want to live anywhere that does not have tulips and elephants and pandas and dogs and redwoods and palm trees and fluffy clouds and green pastures," Kate said, looking out the window. "This planet is amazing."

"And dolphins, manatees, whales, bats, lions, oceans, springs, and forests. It's all worth fighting for. That's why we are going to Texas," Sinclair said.

Kate flipped on the radio, scrolling around for music. When she found a song she liked, she left it there and tried to enjoy it. She wanted to get out of this depressing mood.

After a while, the channel lost reception and Kate scrolled around. She paused to listen to a religious leader with a strong southern accent, praying.

"We pray for the souls of our brothers and sisters lost on July 14. We pray for their loved ones left behind. America, no the world, lost its innocence on July 14. We pray to the Lord to help us find forgiveness for who caused the violent massacre of millions of innocents."

Innocents and lost innocence? I don't think America has ever been innocent, and they all had guns. Once again, Kate did not say what she was thinking. Yvette died that day, and she was not sure if Sinclair was religious; perhaps he found solace in words like the preacher was using. Kate scrolled looking for music.

She paused when an interview caught her attention.

"The final official number seems to be twenty-eight. Twenty-eight souls worldwide were lost to the falling debris yesterday evening. It seems a small number compared to the hundreds of thousands of lives lost due to the COVID virus and the hundreds of millions lost in the mass shooting on July 14, but each of those twenty-eight people had families and friends who are mourning their loss. Right now, on the phone, we have the fiancé of the jogger on the National Mall that was crushed…" Kate kept scrolling until she hit another interview. She knew listening to the fiancé would make her cry.

"My town was located just twenty miles south of Billings, and it no longer exists. Sixty percent of my small town died on July 14. We hardly had any COVID. We considered ourselves lucky to be so isolated. We did not wear masks. We're mostly farmers and ranchers and coal miners. We don't work from home; we work outside, in the world. We went to the grocery store, and we went to the diner and local bars. We lived our lives. But on the morning of July 14, that all changed. Most people around here carry their guns with them in their trucks or cars or on their bodies. We have the right to protect ourselves. We respect our second amendment rights. But now it's like a ghost town," a man said.

"What were they protecting themselves from? What was the fear? Criminals or animals?" the reporter asked.

"I don't know, both maybe," the man replied.

"Was there a high crime rate in your town? Was there illegal drug use that plagues many rural communities? When was the last time someone was attacked by an animal? Or was this mostly just citizens embracing their second amendment rights?" the reporter asked. "We are really trying to take a deep dive into gun ownership in America since the mass shooting."

"We were a safe, small town with everyone knowing and looking after each other. I can't recall a recent animal attack. Maybe it was safe because most everyone had guns. I thought this interview was about what is happening now? I walk around and it's a ghost town. The grocery store is closed. The restaurants and bars are closed. Cattle roam around freely. After the impact and all the funerals, those people who survived, mostly the elderly and children, left town. I walk around to feed abandoned dogs and cats. I need people to come and help. There are so few people working at the coal mine; pretty soon, America may run out of coal. Where is my President? Where is Congress? What are we supposed to do? The damn shooting was almost two months ago, and we need help," the man said, sounding frustrated with both his situation and the interview.

"What would you have the President and Congress do? Provide funds? For what exactly? What would be the most helpful right now?" the reporter asked.

"Maybe not money; we need people. We need people to come back and open the town for business. I mean, shoot, I drive to Billings for groceries. Amazon still delivers here, just takes a lot longer than usual. We have gas because no one is buying it. We need people. We need life back here again," he replied.

"Well, hopefully, people, including the President, are hearing this and can somehow help," the reporter said, thanking the mayor and wrapping up the interview. "We are still waiting for a statement from the President regarding the downed satellites and car. It has been nineteen hours, and all we have so far are tweets stating that the government is looking into it and will punish those that caused it if they were not accidents. Our D.C. correspondent has seen officials from NASA, Space Force, the Joint Chiefs of Staff, Department of Homeland Security, and other cabinet officials come and go from the White House. Several members of congress were shuttled from Capitol Hill to the White House earlier, but no statements from any of them yet. The American public is growing frustrated by the silence. A small crowd demanding answers has formed in front of the White House. As soon as anyone makes a statement, we will bring it to you live," the reporter said before breaking to a commercial.

"They must be struggling with this," Sinclair said. "If I was in charge, I would say it was an accident. Say something hit something. Say a dramatic and unanticipated atmospheric change caused a reaction, and NASA is ensuring it does not happen again. They should not tie it to the mass shooting or Rex. If they do, that could cause massive panic."

"People at NASA and Space Force will know something is up," Kate said.

"Sure, but they are mostly scientists and will want to have a plausible theory to counter the government's approach; they might support the story to buy time for research. Many are scared government employees who won't publicly question their agency or the President. Don't underestimate the fear of losing a job to keep people quiet," Sinclair said.

"I bet the time delay is due to trouble controlling the President. His sycophants created that monster, and I bet they are having a hard time controlling him and the message now. He probably wants to declare war on someone, maybe me, or the Speaker of the House, and they are trying to stop him," Kate said.

"Excellent point," Sinclair said, looking at her and nodding his head. "You probably just nailed the reason for the delay. They're struggling to control that asshole."

Kate hit the scroll button, looking for a good distracting song or interesting interview.

"How about we stop at the next town for lunch? I guess we need a big, busy exit to find an open grocery store. I would also like to walk a bit. Stretch my legs," Sinclair said.

"Sounds good," Kate said, still scrolling on the radio.

"They didn't mention the tool bag. No one has mentioned the $100,000 NASA tool bag. I guess Jack didn't tell anyone. Interesting, because he doesn't strike me as someone who wants to stay out of the limelight. He could be all over CNN with his bag story. Those guys seem to thrive on attention," Kate continued. "You know, the tool bag reminds me of Colorado."

THIRTEEN

Forty-Nine Days After the Shooting

They struck out on a grocery store but found gas and a sandwich shop. They were talking at a picnic table not far from the highway.

"So, tell me about Colorado, Kate," Sinclair said.

Kate's shoulders tensed, and her face drained of color; she hated talking about this, but she and Sinclair had already been through so much. He was helping her, so he deserved to know about it since it kept coming up.

"Right. We were living in Colorado, and I was walking from the school bus drop area into the building. I accidentally tripped over a boy's bag. I landed hard on my butt on his bag. When I was getting up, I looked in the bag and there was a large gun. Like a military gun. Based on the size of the bag, there may have been more than one. I pleaded with the boy to turn around and go home, to leave school. I just panicked and thought to stop a school shooting, I needed to stop him from going into the school. He ignored me and started to walk around me, so I jumped in front of him and got on my knees and begged him to not do anything." Bile rose in Kate's throat as she spoke.

What happened to him on July 14th? Did he kill himself along with all the other gun owners?

"What happened next?" Sinclair asked.

"I kept repeating, 'please go home, everything will be okay.' I was pleading loud enough for him to hear, but no one else around us. He bent down, pulled me up, and whispered in my ear that if I told anyone he would kill me and my family," Kate stopped talking and looked at her sandwich, a wave of nausea hitting her.

Sinclair's eyes were huge as he stared at Kate, but he did not say a word.

Kate took a big swig of water and continued the story. "Some of the kids around us laughed and made remarks like 'get a room' and other juvenile, crude jokes. Then he walked away, back to the bus area. I rushed into school and went to class. That was stupid, I know in hindsight, but I was in seventh grade. After a couple of hours, I ditched school and ran to the elementary school where my mother taught. I told her and the principal, and we called the Sheriff. Eventually, the cops picked up the kid walking down a street. His name was Theo Mast. They did not find his gun. No one was shot or killed," Kate said.

"Damn, Kate. You stopped a school shooter! You were a hero. You are a hero! Thank God you tripped on that bag! What happened to Theo Mast?" Sinclair asked.

Kate shrugged. All these years later, she'd never looked him up on social media. "Nothing happened to him. He convinced the police that I made up the story; maybe it was his parents or their lawyers, someone very clever. He claimed I was in love with him and made it up to get attention. I had never met him before that morning; he was older, and it was a big school. I did not even know his name until that day. He got everyone to believe I was in love with him and lied to hurt him, revenge for not loving me. It was awful."

"Jesus Christ, Kate, that is terrible," Sinclair said, and his eyes flashed anger.

"And my seventh-grade self decided to confront him to tell him to stop lying. I confronted a boy who at one point had a big gun and threatened my life and demanded he stop lying about me while we were on a public street," Kate said.

Sinclair remained silent, riveted by the story.

"His lawyer used it to get a restraining order on me. A few weeks later, my mom and I left Colorado and moved to Florida; we never looked back. The end," Kate said in a lighter voice. She could tell Sinclair was upset. "It was a long time ago, Sinclair. Until Rex showed up, I never even thought about it much."

Sinclair reached for Kate's hands and squeezed them gently.

"I'm so sorry that happened to you, Kate. I'm so angry for you. I want to punch Theo Mast in the face," Sinclair said.

"Maybe after this is over, we should track him down. We ring his doorbell and when he answers, just punch him in the face and say, 'You know what you did!' just like in the movies." Kate tried again to lighten the mood.

They both ate in silence for a few minutes, but Kate's food didn't have any flavor; she struggled to swallow each bite.

"I doubt he had a good life. He was either depressed or a sociopath or had experienced trauma of some sort. I hope like crazy he did not hurt anyone. He needed help, and I hope he got it. Now, I'm wondering if he survived on July 14. Anyway, we should hit the road," Kate said, cleaning up the trash. "Let's find a Target and grocery store now while we have internet. We should find one on our way; I really want clean clothes."

They spent a few minutes mapping a store that would be open when they arrived. It was in a city, so they felt confident they could find a motel there as well.

They got back on the highway with Kate driving.

"It's two hours to Target and for me to stay awake, I have to sing. We have to sing," Kate said.

They spent the next hour singing pop songs, 70s rock, rap and hip hop, and occasionally country. Whenever they hit a song while scrolling that they both knew, they sang loudly.

Kate was lost in the music until she looked in the rearview mirror and saw a wall of black vehicles approaching quickly behind them.

FOURTEEN

Forty-Nine Days After
the Shooting

"Holy shit, Sinclair! What's that?" Kate exclaimed.

Sinclair turned around to look.

"What the hell! Kate, keep your eyes on the road. Just go steady. It looks like several black SUVs are coming up on us fast. Really fast. Just keep driving; we can't outrun them. If they have sirens or block us, we just pull over. This car is old and not built for speed," Sinclair said, still facing the back window.

Am I under arrest? Will Sinclair be charged with abetting a terrorist, given that's what they think I am?

In mere seconds, the vehicles were on their tail. Two were in the left lane and drove alongside Sinclair's car; two others stayed right behind.

"Sinclair, they are on our ass. Can you see who it is?" Kate said, sounding scared.

"No. Black-tinted windows, but the plates seem government-issued. Not cops, per se, but government. Are those diplomatic plates? It's hard to tell," Sinclair said.

Suddenly, the cars alongside took off even faster. They flew down the highway, leaving Kate and Sinclair in their dust. After a couple of minutes, the two vehicles behind them passed and flew by as well. In a flash, they were gone, not even shapes in the distance. Kate and Sinclair were alone on the highway.

"What the hell was that?" Sinclair said again. "Why did they do that? Why ride up on us like that and not pull us over or give any indication of who they are or what they want?"

Kate kept glancing at the rearview mirror, and Sinclair kept turning around, both breathless from the excitement.

"Guess they weren't looking for us," Kate said. "Did we just let some random government assholes scare the shit out of us?"

"I doubt that was a coincidence," Sinclair responded. "It can't be possible, right?"

"Maybe something else happened, and they are on the way to it. Maybe something else crashed from space or there was violence," Kate said, scrolling on the radio for news. "It sucks having no internet out here."

They drove in silence for the last hour to the Target. They took turns scrolling around the radio. They would pause and listen briefly to heartbreaking interviews with people who had lost so much in the pandemic or shooting or both. They heard interviews with people terrified of gas or food shortages.

"It's all so horrible and sad, but we can't turn it off. We need to know if something new has happened," Kate said.

FIFTEEN

Forty-Nine Days After the Shooting

A few hours later, Kate was in a motel room dumping out her purchases on a bed.

"Target was a total success. Look at these," she said, showing Sinclair her loot. "Clean shorts, clean socks, clean bra, clean undies, cute clean t-shirts, Birk sandal knockoffs, a little make-up, some real moisturizer, and a real brush. Healthy snacks too. A well-deserved shopping distraction. I can't wait to take a shower and put on clean clothes."

Kate was committed to finding some levity despite the stressful situation they were in.

"And the fancy grocery store dinner was so good after sub sandwiches three times in a row," Sinclair said as he put groceries in the mini-fridge, including a new and much better bottle of wine. "And we have a healthy breakfast tomorrow. Now, I need to charge everything and get some work done."

"I'm going to take my stuff to my room and go for a walk. Get a little exercise and make some phone calls," Kate said, putting her loot back into the bag.

Kate felt safer in this town. She saw at least twenty people at Target with two cashier lines open. Very quiet for a Target but busy enough that people weren't watching her. Same at the grocery store, with a dozen cars in the lot. The total ghost town of the previous night felt like a horror movie. This felt like a pandemic. And because there were a few other guests here, the hotel reception woman was not particularly interested in them. Still, Kate waited in the car during their initial check-in, wearing her hat, sunglasses, and mask as a precaution.

Her face might be all over the news.

"Be careful, Kate. Stay in the parking lot. We have no idea where those SUVs went or what that was about. That was weird and made me nervous," Sinclair said as he sat down in front of his computer. "Well, this is interesting, very interesting," Sinclair said, looking at the screen. "Claudia sent some codes. She thinks they might help us get past Yvette's security walls." Sinclair started typing fast.

"I'll let you work," Kate said before exiting for her room next door.

She deposited her stuff on the bed and walked out into the evening heat. It was really hot, but it felt good to pace the large, mostly vacant parking lot. Normally, she'd want to go for a run, but, instead, she walked in circles around the large lot.

She called Kyle to quickly touch base. As she was about to say goodbye, she saw a sign indicating that there was a pool behind the motel. "I love you, Kyle. Will call you in the morning," Kate said, hustling around back to check out the pool.

Kate squealed when she saw the cute, small pool. She used her room key to get through the fence. There were only three other cars in the parking lot, so with the motel almost empty, the pool was as well. It looked clean and smelled like chlorine, so she took off her shoes and put her feet in. It was still around 90 degrees, so the water felt good; Kate smiled in pleasure as she walked laps in the shallow end.

Her phone rang.

"Hi, Mom, how are you?" Kate asked.

"Good, Kate. Making progress. We should get to where we need to be in Tennessee before dark tomorrow or the next day. Play it by ear. The kids have good hours and moody hours; sometimes they love each other and sometimes they fight. It's crazy. But we're making progress. Where are you?"

"We are in North Carolina at a nice motel. I'm walking laps in a small hotel pool while talking to you. Right this minute, everything is okay," Kate said.

"Good. Kate, that is great. I am so sorry, but I have not watched the video yet. I will try in a little while when the kids are settled in bed. They are a handful, and I want to give it my full attention when I watch it." Kate's mom added, "I am really sorry; I am dying to know what's been going on."

"No worries, Mom. Seriously. Focus on the kids and driving. It's a lot. I'm just happy knowing you have it. Watch it after you hand the kids over and you have space in your head and time on your hands.

Seriously. Watching it today or tomorrow or the day after will not make any difference," Kate explained.

"Okay, I am going to go for now. I love you. You and Sinclair stay healthy and safe. Whatever this latest nightmare is, it will pass. You are so brave and strong, Kate. Every little thing is gonna be alright," her mom said.

"Thanks, Mom. I love you," Kate said before hanging up.

She walked a few more little laps in the pool. "Well, screw it," Kate said, putting her phone on the pool ledge and diving under in her clothes.

Kate swam several laps in the little pool but was startled when a shadow appeared above her, causing her to snort water up her nose.

"Hey, Sinclair. You scared me," Kate said, coughing and laughing.

"I got worried when I realized you were not walking around the parking lot. You just disappeared. This is a nice find. Cute pool," Sinclair said. "I didn't mean to scare you. I'm just being overly cautious. Still a little freaked about those SUVs on the highway. And, you know, things falling from the sky."

Kate flipped on her back and swam an easy lap, watching Sinclair. "Or getting snatched up by Rex. That could happen."

"Yes, that is true," Sinclair agreed.

"Want to come in? It's small but refreshing. Fun," Kate said, still doing a gentle backstroke.

"No thanks. I just wanted to be sure you were okay," Sinclair said.

"Make any progress with the information Claudia sent?" Kate asked.

"Yes, I did. Got into some encrypted files. It seems there is debris from the collision, and Yvette knew where it was. I believe she may have seen it or even touched it," Sinclair said, sounding excited. "But I can't figure out where it is. It must be in Houston, but it does not seem to be at Johnson. I need to keep digging."

"I have complete faith you will find it," Kate said, swimming another leisurely lap.

"Leaving you here, I worry that something could happen to you, and I would not know it," Sinclair said.

"Oh, I'm sorry. You're right; we should stick close together," Kate said, climbing out of the pool. "I didn't mean for you to worry."

"Anything on the news?" Kate asked Sinclair as they walked back to their rooms. Kate was dripping wet since she didn't have a towel. She moved away from Sinclair to shake out her hair like a dog without splattering him with water.

"Nothing. No new violence. No new objects crashing down from space. Just a normal day during a global pandemic," Sinclair said. "Would you like some wine?"

"Please. But I am going to drink it next door since I'm dripping wet," Kate said.

Sinclair gave her a towel and a cup of wine. "Then let's say good night. Get up and hit the road early," he said as Kate turned and walked to her room.

"Thanks, Sinclair. Goodnight!" Kate called over her shoulder.

She appreciated that Sinclair worried about her and was so honest about his feelings. Again, she was filled with gratitude for his friendship and help with this nightmare. She showered and was asleep before she knew it, without finishing the wine or turning on the TV.

SIXTEEN

Fifty Days After the Shooting

They were on the road and discussing Yvette's fire-walls by 8:00 a.m.

"I was up most of the night trying but did not learn much. It feels strange trying to break into my wife's files. We are lucky she was double-dipping or everything would be in NASA or corporate hands. Her manner of doing business meant she treated everything as though it was hers to protect and conceal. However, without the codes from Claudia, we would have nothing. Actually, we still have nothing. I'll work on it again tonight. Even though I got into some of the files, I just don't understand what I am seeing. There are coordinates, but I think they might be in code. They do not indicate NASA Johnson Space Center, but if they're purposefully written to be confusing, they could be anywhere at the Center or nearby. If I can't crack it on the road, hopefully being there and talking to people she worked with will help," Sinclair explained.

"You'll figure it out," Kate said, offering some encouragement. He was working so arduously; she had no idea what she would do without him. He was doing most of the driving, the research, and paying for everything. Most importantly, he believed in her. He gave her hope that something could be done even though there was no logical reason to feel it. They were not cleaning up the dangerous pollution in space, and she knew that Rex knew it.

Kate took his hand, squeezed it, and said, "I am so grateful for you. I would have no idea what to do. You were with me when that car crashed down. You being with me when those strange cars passed us yesterday. I am just so grateful for you, and I appreciate you. Oh, and I promise I will pay you back."

"Thanks, Kate. I am happy to be here rather than going crazy at home alone. I would be alone trying to put things together without your experiences and first-hand information. You know I am very curious to see where this goes. To see what Rex is and why he is doing what he is doing. I'm very happy to be here on this adventure. And please forget about the money. Seriously, do not think about it again. Yvette and I make, made, good money. Work was our life, so we didn't spend much on cars or homes or travel. Besides, not having kids is a huge way to save money. Friends tell me it costs around $30,000 a year for school and activities in D.C., and that is little kids, not including college. I can easily afford a road trip to Texas. Please don't worry about it," Sinclair said, squeezing her hand.

"College is incredibly expensive. I have so much debt, I can't even think about grad school," Kate said.

They both jumped when Kate's phone rang.

"Unlisted number. Probably spam," Kate said, looking at it and hanging up.

Kate put the radio on and started scrolling when the phone rang again. She turned up the radio and silenced the call.

"I love this song," Kate said, singing along. "It's sad and reminds me of high school in Florida."

The phone rang again.

Kate stared at the unlisted number scrolling across the screen and thought about putting the phone where she could not see it, but then had a strange feeling.

She decided to answer it. She pushed speaker and looked at Sinclair; he knew to be quiet, and she did not say a word.

There was almost a full minute of silence.

"Good morning, Kate, Sinclair. Thank you for the far more enjoyable night. If we had to sleep in the car again, I was going to shoot someone. Just kidding of course!" Jo-Ellen said with a snarky laugh.

"Jo-Ellen?" Kate asked.

Jo-Ellen was the Space Force agent who had eavesdropped on her and Sinclair's backyard conversation about Rex and space debris. She had warned Kate that Space Force was going to toss her under the bus by indicating she had something to do with the mass shooting. Despite that, Kate did not know where Jo-Ellen's loyalty lay, and she did not trust her.

"Yes, it's me," Jo-Ellen said.

"What do you mean, 'sleep in a car'? Where are you?" Kate asked.

"Girl, when you locked on that Target, I knew where you were going. We flew passed you on the highway. I had to pee like a racehorse in heat, and your quest for clean clothes allowed me to get to a nice hotel, pee in a toilet, and send Malcolm off to watch you shop. Much more pleasant than the shithole truck stop motel you picked the night before. We had to sleep in our cars off the highway. Don't think I will ever forgive you for that. Jesus. Heat, mosquitoes, sleeping in cars. It has to end, Kate," Jo-Ellen said. "Though I will say your faces were priceless when we passed you. You looked terrified! I shouldn't think it was funny, but it was. We all had a good laugh. After that motel and sleeping in the car, well, you kind of deserved it."

"What? I don't understand. Are you following us?" Kate asked, looking over her shoulder.

"Of course we are, Kate. You are heading to Houston. You are not supposed to know, but I assumed you knew we are tracking you. We're not supposed to let you out of our sight or let you see us, but after that empty motel and no other accommodations for miles, well that's not going to happen again. The heads up on your Target destination last night was much better. We did not let you out of our sight, well not for long, and you never saw us, and we all slept in beds. Everyone is happy. Space Force is happy. You and Sinclair are happy on your road trip. I'm happy for now. All is well," Jo-Ellen said.

"Okay. I guess. So, why are you calling?" Kate asked.

"Just keep letting me know where you plan to stop. Google it. Pick towns with more than one hotel. We will all make it to Texas healthy and happy. Well, unless something from space falls out of the sky on you. I think there is another car up there, or some other new kind of violence," Jo-Ellen said. "Bye for now."

SEVENTEEN

Fifty Days After the Shooting

"**W**e figured they were tracking us. Maybe they are just a few miles behind us now," Kate said, glancing over her shoulder. "Space Force should be focusing on the dangerous pollution, not me; I can't stop the violence.

"Yes, we knew they were following us. I guess we just ignore them," Sinclair said, turning on the radio. He found a news channel, and the President was speaking.

"They came crashing down. Two satellites owned by the US government. Each one is worth more than 300 million dollars. They landed so close to the White House; many people think I was the target. They screwed up and hit the National Mall, not me and my family. Guess they aren't so smart. However, there are others at NASA and Space Force that think something hit them and knocked them out of orbit and it was an accident. We shall see. We shall see. There is an ongoing investigation. I have also talked to Chinese and Russian leaders to see what fell there and how close to their homes. The whole thing is fishy. They say their scientists also think it was some strange accident. Maybe solar or stellar flares disabled them. I guess it has happened before. That is what the scientists say anyway. But my government is investigating, and we will get to the bottom of it very, very soon. I also want to say if they were shot down intentionally and if I was the target, then that is an act of war and Space Force, or our regular Earth-bound military will strike back, and they won't know what hit them. They won't know what hit them! I don't have time for questions because I need to be briefed about something else now."

"That was the brief statement the President made earlier this morning from the Rose Garden. The President and his staff were not wearing masks, forcing many of the reporters present to socially distance themselves. This made it difficult to press him to answer questions. The President did not mention the twenty-eight people killed by the falling equipment. We have requested interviews with experts from NASA and Space Force and expect that to happen soon. When it does, we will break from programming to bring it to you live. Currently, it seems to be another unexplained and deadly phenomenon in this most unusual year. More news on the hour," the reporter said as a block of advertisements started.

"That was interesting. They seemed to keep him somewhat on message. But his followers will only hear that he was targeted, which means there is a bad guy somewhere that is responsible. The nut-bags will think Antifa or Black Lives Matter or some psychotic, baby-eating Democrat or me. Let's look at Twitter," Kate said, turning down the radio and the overly loud commercials.

"Funny, but he is actually right and speaking the truth. No one really knows what happened. I mean, he flips things around and is doing it now. He's creating confusion and doubt, but in this case, he's right. There is confusion. You know, he often speaks the truth, his truth anyway. I mean, he says when he is cheating or lying, and he brags about getting away with it," Sinclair said.

"I wonder if he is struggling to find a way to make all this work for him politically. He denied the pandemic and refuses to wear a mask, which excites and emboldens his followers. He loves to blame the Democrats and press for over-hyping the virus. Ironic for a man who exaggerates everything about himself. But how can he make the shooting and the satellites work for him? Sadly, so many of his party, supporters, and family died on July 14. Maybe he is struggling," Kate said. "Has he even talked about all the empty towns like that one in Montana? We heard that gentleman asking for help, specifically asking the President for help. It's all so sad."

"Let's listen to some music to pass the time," Sinclair said.

They listened to music for an hour, occasionally singing.

Kate wanted to do a search for a good grocery store up ahead, but she did not want to give Jo-Ellen any satisfaction.

I'm not sure I want to work with Jo-Ellen. I don't trust her or Space Force.

Kate turned down the radio.

"Sinclair, have you ever seen a UFO or unidentified aerial phenomena or anything to prove there is life out there beyond us?" Kate asked.

Sinclair swallowed hard and did not take his eyes from the road. "There have been many pictures of objects that indicate some kind of technology has come very close to Earth. There have been materials collected from all over the world that can't be explained. We usually say they were found on an asteroid, but not all of them were. The U.S. government doesn't want to scare Americans or let other hostile nations know that we have found carbon-based materials not linked to anything on Earth. The general consensus among officials is to tell the world when we know more; so far, we don't know anything for sure." Sinclair briefly turned and looked at Kate. "They have found minerals that are not on our periodic table."

Kate got goosebumps all over from excitement. She always thought it would be weird for Earth to be the only planet with life.

"Wow, I'm not surprised. It's so exciting and amazing that it's been kept secret. Most of the people who know are scientists or at least had been until the rise of corporate space. I can see scientists keeping secrets, wanting to know more before they draw conclusions," Kate said.

"Most of the space centers and active research locations are surrounded by military bases and installations. Originally, back in the 1950s when it all started, it was to protect space exploration and activities from the Russians. Now, it's to keep the secrets from other countries, the press, and Americans. All that security has worked. Well, until this President with his big mouth and Rex with his awesome power," Sinclair said.

He continued, "We have been experiencing millions of tons of superheated gas from the surface of the sun, thrown 90 million miles toward Earth. Coronal mass ejections have been increasing significantly. Down here on Earth, we don't feel them, at least not yet. But the geomagnetic waves unleashed by solar storms can destroy power grids, jam radio communications, cover people on airplanes in dangerous levels of radiation, and knock critical satellites off-kilter. Space weather is almost as important as Earth weather. That's why the solar flares story is entirely plausible. The objects and locations of the crashes are the strange curves in this situation, which have to be linked to Rex. Also, the fact that they didn't burn up has to be Rex too. Unfortunately, even without Rex, Space is becoming far more dangerous."

"The pollution is making space more dangerous just like here on Earth. Pollution is making this planet toxic. It's killing people and nature, and we depend on each other. The pollution pissed off Rex; now hundreds of millions of people are dead. Our irresponsible and selfish behavior screws up everything beautiful and natural and wonderful. Will we ever learn?" Kate asked rhetorically.

Yvette's phone rang, interrupting their conversation. It was in the console and took her a moment of fumbling around to get it. Kate hit speaker and held it close to Sinclair's head.

"Hello," Sinclair answered.

"Hi, Sinclair. It's Claudia. How are you?" she asked.

"I'm good. Just driving. How are you?" Sinclair asked.

"I'm okay, I guess. Have you had a chance to use those codes I sent?" Claudia jumped into work, all business.

"Yes. Thank you. They were so helpful. I got around some of Yvette's firewalls and found some interesting coordinates. We're just not sure where they are yet." Sinclair winced for saying "we".

"Oh, you still have Yvette's assistant with you? What's her name again?" Claudia asked.

"Katie. She is right here. We're on speaker," Sinclair said.

"Where are you? Where are you driving to?" Claudia sounded suspicious.

"We decided to head to Texas to check Yvette's office at Johnson and meet with some of her contacts," Sinclair replied.

"Driving to Texas during a pandemic sounds extremely dangerous. That makes my find even better for you, a little safer," Claudia said.

"What did you find?" Sinclair asked.

"Those coordinates are in code. It was an old code from way back when that I knew Yvette to use. She had projects that she wanted me and a few others to understand, but not necessarily her supervisors. Yvette was such a badass; she made up her own rules and lived her own way. No reverence for hierarchy or seniority or tradition," Claudia said, sighing loudly. "I miss her so much."

"Me too, Claudia. Me too. What did the code tell you about the coordinates?" Sinclair asked, getting her back on track.

"They are in Florida, not Texas. You need to head south," Claudia said.

EIGHTEEN

Fifty Days After the Shooting

"I have to go, Sinclair. Call me when you are online, and I will walk you through the code. Stay safe out there," Claudia said and ended the call.

"Florida. Interesting," Sinclair said.

"We need to get off at the next exit and find a paper map or person who can direct us to I-95. I don't want to type it anywhere. What Jo-Ellen doesn't know won't kill her. It will piss her off though," Kate said with a smile.

"She'll figure it out," Sinclair said, looking up in the sky. "I bet they have satellites on us."

"Sure, but I like the idea that she feels in control but is not. I'm not helping Space Force after they set me up to take the blame. She can be confused and struggle for a few minutes; she deserves that. Plus, she laughed about scaring us yesterday on the highway, which is some total mean-girl bullshit," Kate said, watching for exits with larger gas stations. "She might think we are getting off for lunch and fly past us; that would be awesome."

After a while, they stopped at a service station that had public restrooms but little else. They parked near a huge, idling truck. Kate saw two men speaking to each other near the restroom, and since there were no other cars in the lot, she assumed they were the truck drivers. As Sinclair headed into the building, Kate walked over to the men.

"Excuse me, sorry to interrupt, but can you tell me how to get to I-95 from here?" Kate asked.

"Sure, but why don't you use your phone?" one guy asked. Both men put masks on as Kate approached.

"Battery is draining fast," Kate said. "Especially if I use GPS."

"It's easy. Are you going north or south?" one of the men asked.

"South," Kate replied.

The guy slowly walked her through the various highways and turns to get to I-95. "Should take you about 90 minutes to get there."

Kate typed the directions into her phone.

"Thank you so much. And thank you for your service; you guys are frontline heroes and taking so much risk to keep America going. I mean it sincerely: thank you."

"I'm just a rookie, learning. We're brothers, and my younger brother here is my teacher," the second man said.

"Yeah, so many truckers shot themselves in July that my company is desperate and hiring any old loser at this point," he said, clearly teasing his brother. Kate could tell he was smiling through his mask. "If you are looking for a job, call that number," he said, pointing to the truck. "They're giving signing bonuses and really good pay."

"I may have recently lost my job," Kate said, taking a picture of the company name and number. "I'm sorry if you lost friends and family in the mass shooting."

"We lost so many friends, and I lost so many colleagues," the trucker said. Both men nodded their heads the same way. "We were lucky that we didn't lose any immediate family."

"We're Quakers," the brothers added simultaneously by way of explanation.

"Oh. That's interesting. I guess I did not realize Quakers still lived by the no-violence rule. I mean, many practitioners of many religions don't follow the tenants or commandments or rules anymore. Sorry, I don't mean to be disrespectful." Kate felt like she had put her foot in her mouth.

"No offense taken. We know many Christians have guns and support different forms of violence from the seemingly endless wars to the death penalty. But we don't, and we were very lucky on July 14. I guess our faith saved us," the trucker said.

Sinclair came over after patiently waiting near the building. "Kate, we need to hit the road."

"Sure. Okay. Thanks, gentlemen, for the directions and job suggestion. Stay safe!" Kate said.

"You stay safe as well. The roads and towns are empty, so if you run into trouble, you might not be able to find help," one of the brothers called out so Sinclair could also hear.

As they got in the car Sinclair said, "I hung back because I'm a man and Black, and I thought they would be nicer to you alone. When I heard the Quaker conversation, I realized I shouldn't judge a book by its cover."

"In this case, no. I was surprised as well. I'm sure your judgment has kept you safe, so maybe don't stop doing it," Kate responded. "I got directions; 95 is about 90 minutes away. Wonder how long before Jo-Ellen figures out we changed directions?"

"Probably immediately. They may have put an old-fashioned tracker on the car. I don't have OnStar or ATX, so I'm not sure that they hear our actual conversations unless they added a bug last night. They can track our phones since they knew about Target. It's ridiculous that our phones provide such easy access for the government and Google to track us, but many Americans claim wearing a mask takes away their freedom. Morons. Thanks to technology, none of us have privacy or freedom," Sinclair said.

"You can't entirely blame them. The President and others feed them lies that hurt them. It's sad. Just like climate change. They might lose their jobs, homes, health, or even lives due to extreme weather, but the President and their leaders continue to lie to people and claim it's not happening so corporate America and the rich get richer. It's cruel manipulation and a violation of trust. I mean, there is a reason to lie about climate change, so that the rich can get richer. But what is the reason to lie and tell them not to wear masks? It just increases their chance of getting the virus and for what? Not votes because so many are dying. It's really, really sad," Kate added.

"I think we need some music," Sinclair said, scrolling around. He stumbled on a cover of Marvin Gaye's "What's Going On?"

Kate squealed with excitement.

"This is the perfect song for this moment," Sinclair said as they sang along.

NINETEEN

Fifty Days After the Shooting

S inclair drove for another hour, listening to music. Kate was lost in thought.

"Hopefully the junction to 95 has a grocery store or someplace for lunch. Being vegan can be a pain during road trips under normal circumstances, and the pandemic closings are making it harder. You would think getting fruits and vegetables would not be so hard in this day and age. You would think eating healthy and getting strong would be a shared empowering message during a pandemic," Kate said, suddenly interrupted by her ringing phone.

"Oh, she must know that we took a detour," Kate said, seeing the unlisted number appear. "Let's let her wait a bit. Remember, she scared us and laughed at us."

Kate muted the phone as it continued to flash unlisted number, over and over.

"Put her out of her misery, Kate," Sinclair said, laughing.

Kate answered, clicked on speaker, but did not say a word.

"Where are you going, Kate? I thought we agreed to communicate. Now we are doubling back at high speeds. Someone might get hurt," Jo-Ellen said, sounding very angry.

"It's not our fault you're going the wrong way. It's not our fault you made the bonehead decision to get in front of us. And it certainly would not be our fault if you are in an accident or hurt anyone. Jesus Christ, is no one at Space Force capable of taking responsibility for their actions?" Kate asked.

Jo-Ellen sighed loudly before saying, "I take my eyes off you for less than an hour, and now what? You are heading to I-95? Why? Where are you going? We are going to catch up and have to tail you now; this will be so incredibly annoying for all of us."

Kate said nothing.

"We are on our way," Jo-Ellen said.

"Has Space Force organized a cleanup? What are they doing to address the dangerous pollution? We are past the five-day deadline," Kate said, thinking of Rex's last warning.

"I don't know; I'm busy following you. We are just hoping Rex doesn't have another temper tantrum. He could just as easily hit you as anyone. The roadster was pretty close," Jo-Ellen said.

Kate looked at Sinclair, and he shrugged.

"Oh, I am not worried about Rex hurting us. I mean, apparently, he could. He could easily kill us, but I don't think he will. I did what he asked. In fact, I did exactly what he asked. Has Space Force?" Kate asked coolly. She was not going to let Jo-Ellen upset her.

"Like I said, I don't know. I'm too busy chasing you," Jo-Ellen responded.

"Check in with your bosses, all those acting generals, and find out what they are doing about the pollution. Call me back, tell me their plan, and maybe then I will tell you where Sinclair and I are going."

With that, Kate hung up.

TWENTY

Fifty Days After the Shooting

They got fast food at the I-95 junction and ate it in the car. They were the only customers at the restaurant, and long moments would go by without seeing another car on any of the surrounding roads. It was just a highway pitstop, and it seemed very lonely to Kate.

"As we move south, there are fewer and fewer cars and people. I did not notice the lack of people in D.C. very much, mostly because everyone stayed indoors due to the pandemic. Until now, I thought it felt like a horror movie. There are people, but they are mostly in hiding. Just a skeleton crew going to work. Now it's starting to feel really empty, post-apocalyptic. I don't think those store and restaurant chains over there are ever open," Kate said, waving to a different road with a strip mall.

"We have not seen a police car since we left D.C. Not one," Sinclair said.

"Huh, I hadn't noticed before, but you're right. It's all so strange. I logically know why there are no cops, but it just seems so incredibly strange," Kate said.

"I am sad for all the people who died and their loved ones in mourning, but I am fine with fewer police. One less thing to worry about," Sinclair added, biting into his bean burrito.

Back on the highway, they decided to power through to the Florida border. Kate was driving and scrolling on the radio to stay awake. She skipped over music looking for news.

"I have always been a news addict," Kate said. "Even before the pandemic. I was raised reading the newspaper every day. Still do. And I love *60 Minutes*. I think I am the only person of my generation to ever say that. My mom and I would watch it every Sunday night when I was a kid."

"Whoa, go back. I recognize that voice," Sinclair said.

"The Administration, the federal government leadership, has been incompetent on all fronts since before the pandemic started. However, with so many political appointees dead from the shooting, Congress and the federal government are working more closely together than ever before to get through this crisis. We have to. And it's working," said the Speaker of the House of Representatives.

"I like her," Sinclair said.

The reporter or moderator spoke next. "We also have with us Jane Summers, the Acting Administrator of the Environmental Protection Agency. So, you are saying Speaker, that you are directly working with the

EPA? Not going through the traditional executive branch channels?"

"Exactly. My staff and I speak with Jane almost daily on conference calls. It's not just about obtaining funding or moving money around; this is far more hands-on work," said the Speaker.

"Would you give us an example, Jane?" the reporter asked.

"Of course, but first let me clarify that I am not sure I am officially Acting; we are still waiting for an official announcement. The Office of Water was flooded with calls from municipalities across the country, as well as panic-stricken congressional hill staff. Many employees at drinking water systems had been killed in the mass shooting, and people were concerned that the drinking water was no longer safe. Some of the deceased had worked at the large systems, and many, many more worked at the small systems. Some rural systems had no staff to continue monitoring and treating their water. So, I reached out to EPA management at headquarters and regional offices, inquiring if they had staff who could do emergency frontline work. We sent EPA staff out to the field to work at the treatment facilities to make sure they were providing safe drinking water."

"So, office staff, the regulation writing people, are now doing fieldwork?" the moderator asked for clarification.

"Exactly," Jane replied. "We asked them to evaluate if sudden and dramatic population declines due to the shooting would impact treatment since the amount of water that flows through pipes is very important.

Sending staff who work in offices dealing with data and laws, out into the field raised some legal concerns, which I communicated to the Speaker. The cool thing is that we decided to forgo government procedure temporarily to make it happen, and it has been working really well. It also worked for the management of some Superfund sites and some non-drinking water and air quality monitoring. We focused on what could be immediately dangerous if neglected, even for a short term, or could cause serious public health problems down the road. EPA staff is seeing and calling in unanticipated problems, so we can find solutions together. Kind of like what FEMA does after a natural disaster, but the mass shooting was far too widespread for just one agency. We all need to work together, and we are."

"Very interesting. It must have been exciting for regulators to be in the field, actually implementing their regulations," the moderator said.

"Yes, and we were fortunate that the EPA lost fewer staff lives than any other federal agency on July 14. It seems engineers, chemists, and environmentalists are less likely to own guns. Now, we are all just working together the best we can to keep America's public health environment safe," Jane explained.

"And we are doing this with all the agencies. We have people at the Department of Agriculture sending D.C. and regional office staff to inspect slaughterhouses and work on the ground with farmers to keep healthy food flowing. We lost so many farmers in the shooting. We have staff at the Department of Interior working on oil platforms and managing our National

Wildlife Refuges and National Parks. Government employees have stepped up and out into the world. It's been amazing," the Speaker interjected.

A man's voice broke into the discussion. Kate figured he must have been introduced before they started listening.

"At the Department of Transportation, where airplanes, trains, barges, etc. need to be monitored and inspected, our staff has been able to work efficiently due to so few people traveling; basically, moving consumer goods is the only crucial thing happening. Because of the pandemic, and having lost 70,000,000 Americans in one day, we can hold our transportation systems together safely for now. But everything has changed. Everything," the man said.

"Yes, that is absolutely true with all the agencies. If we had not lost more than twenty percent of our population, we would not have the staff to hold the critically important infrastructure together…" Jane's voice was lost to static.

Kate turned the dial on the radio, trying to find it on another channel, but it was gone.

"They will replay it, or we can find it online when we get to a hotel tonight," Kate said. "Nice to know some agencies and their staff are stepping up to fill the void and save lives. Unlike Space Force, which is more focused on blaming me."

She'd never forgive her employers for treating her like a criminal. If she managed to get out of this situation alive and without landing in federal prison, she was looking for another job. She liked being on the road; maybe truck driving wouldn't be so bad if she could manage to stay awake.

Kate flipped her attention from the road to the radio, not noticing the fleet of SUVs on her tail until they were quite close.

"Oh shit, Sinclair, we have company! I hope that is Jo-Ellen and Space Force!" Kate exclaimed.

Sinclair's head whipped around to see what Kate saw in the rearview mirror. Several black SUVs were coming up fast. Within seconds, they were behind, beside, and in front of their car.

Kate was squeezing the steering wheel tightly.

It could be Jo-Ellen and Malcolm—or it could be worse.

"What if it's another agency? FBI? CIA? They could drive us off the road and no one would ever know," Kate said nervously.

"Just drive steadily, Kate. It must be Space Force," Sinclair said. "Who else would be this entitled and obnoxious? We haven't broken the law."

"And they aren't the law!" Kate said, pissed. "Can you see Malcolm or Jo-Ellen in the cars?"

"The windows are really tinted; just keep driving. Try to ignore them," Sinclair responded.

They drove boxed in on the highway for another hour. Occasionally, another car would appear, and the SUVs would clear a path to allow it to pass. Same for the huge trucks, but some of the truck drivers slowed down and strained their necks to see what was happening.

"This is obnoxious and dangerous," Kate said. "It's calling attention to us. It will bring reporters, perhaps dangerous mob attention, that we don't deserve. I'm going to pull over and tell them to go fuck themselves," Kate said as she slowed down. "I don't want anyone to get hurt, not even these assholes. Now they're making me swear, which is really pissing me off."

Just as Kate got below 30 mph, the SUVs sped up and flew past them off into the distance. Kate gave them the middle finger as they drove by.

TWENTY-ONE

Fifty Days After the Shooting

They pulled off the highway and checked into a motel about 30 minutes from the Florida border. They were in the same room. Kate was sitting on a bed, eating a salad, and watching the news. Sinclair was at the table eating a sandwich while working on Yvette's codes.

Sinclair called Claudia and put her on speaker. "Hey, Claudia. I see the codes, your work, and how it relates to Yvette's system, but then I get confused; these coordinates are all over the place. Some are in Texas. Some in Louisiana. Some are in Mexico. Most seem to be in Florida. Is that why you said we should head to Florida?"

Kate stopped chewing. *What if Claudia isn't on our side after all and is trying to send us on the wrong trail?*

"I read it as these are coordinates for the different pieces that fell to Earth. Must have been a massive collision. I'm not sure if Yvette was given the locations and then she encrypted the information, or if it came encrypted. I also can't tell where she got the information. Maybe she found it? Maybe she actually located the debris? She did travel a lot over the past year. She was working like a dog doing serious overtime. Someone may have given her all this information. I just can't figure it out," Claudia explained. "All the debris was moved to Florida, as indicated in the final codes I sent you. It seems like someone collected it and took it there."

"Claudia, this is amazing work. You should brand yourself the new Yvette and get her gigs!" Sinclair said.

"Maybe I will. What do I have to lose?" Claudia said, suddenly sounding sad.

"Okay, so where exactly in Florida is the debris being stored?" Sinclair asked. "The obvious place would be Kennedy Space Center, but is that too obvious?"

"I think it's there. Some might still be at Eglin or another military base, but most coordinates lead to Brevard County," Claudia said.

"Who collected it? Military? NASA? How did they hide this massive operation?" Sinclair asked.

"I have no idea. Hopefully, you will find answers in Florida," Claudia responded. "I'll keep digging here, but it seems the vast amount of her files involved locating the debris and tracking it; I'm not sure how much more I can help."

"Claudia, you have been an enormous help. You have no idea. We can't thank you enough," Sinclair said. "We will keep you in the loop when we find out more."

"Take me off speaker, Sinclair," Claudia said.

The prickling sensation on the back of Kate's neck intensified.

Sinclair turned up the volume as he turned off the speaker. Kate moved her head very close to Sinclair so she could still hear Claudia.

"Sure," Sinclair said, "what's up?"

"Is Katie still with you?" Claudia asked.

"Yes, she is. We are working on this together," Sinclair said.

"That's nice. It's really none of my business, but I knew you and Yvette were separating. I would ask her if it bothered you that she was gone so often, and she would just shrug. I wasn't sure what that meant, or if it meant that she didn't care either way. It made me sad because I like both of you a lot; you were such a great couple. I think your relationship simply ran its course. It seemed to end naturally and without any anger or recriminations. Nothing like my loud, messy divorce. Of course, we had kids," Claudia said, sighing.

Kate relaxed a little. If Claudia wanted to talk about their marriages, it made sense to do so privately.

"I can't imagine your loss, Claudia. When I think of your brilliant, funny, kind, full-of-life boys, it just breaks me. I am so sorry for all your loss," Sinclair said, tears in his eyes.

"Yes, it is the worst pain imaginable. Every day, I wake up with the pain, and it stays with me all day. Then at night, it comes in my dreams," Claudia said with another sad sigh before clearing her throat loudly. "I don't care that you are dating so soon; another pretty space junkie with complicated and mysterious employers seems your type," Claudia said.

Kate realized she should move away; this was intimate and none of her business. *Maybe Sinclair and I are getting too close.* Although, she was very curious to hear what Sinclair would say.

Sinclair's brows furrowed as he said, "We are colleagues and friends working on an important project. We aren't dating."

If Claudia thinks we're a couple, do others? What is Kyle thinking?

"Oh right, okay. Were you friends before July 14?" Claudia asked.

"No, not really. She helped me with Yvette's death, and we became friends," Sinclair said. "She was with me when I found Yvette."

Sinclair took a deep breath and tried to end the conversation. "We'll keep you in the loop as we move forward. This information is very helpful. Like I said, we can't thank you enough."

"Okay, sounds good. Oh, wait, Sinclair, what is Katie's last name?" Claudia asked.

Kate's heart started pounding.

Sinclair quickly hung up the phone and looked at Kate. "Claudia knows."

TWENTY-TWO

Fifty Days After the Shooting

Sinclair kept tracking debris on his computer, and Kate walked around the parking lot, checking in with her mom and Kyle. Her mom told her she still had not listened to the recording because things were a little messy in Tennessee. Kyle said he missed her and was enjoying working with the cops to keep the neighborhood safe.

Kate worried Claudia would tell the media where they were heading. It was so hot, so Kate went to her room to shower and change. She paced the small room, checking texts, Slack, Twitter, Facebook, and emails. When she felt up to date, she headed next door to Sinclair's room.

"Anything new?" she asked as she retrieved the wine bottle which had moved with them from the last hotel. She poured what was left into two cups hoping it would ease her anxiety.

"Yes, I have been able to backtrack and see where and how the debris was moved after it landed. I can tell the size of some of it by the size of the trucks and ships sent to retrieve it, and it does all seem to be heading to Florida. So far, it looks like tons, not pounds. Some of this came down dangerously large. It's a miracle they kept it covered up and no one was hurt," Sinclair responded. "I can't wait to see what it is."

Kate flopped down on one of the beds.

"I can't wait to see if it's useful to managing or stopping the Rex situation. I pray to all the gods," Kate said, dramatically squeezing her eyes shut, "that this leads us to a way to stop further violence. I am putting positive energy into the universe. No more anger or swear words, just pure love, so we can prevent more pain and death."

Sinclair did not respond; he was busy on the computer.

As Kate sipped her wine, she flipped channels with the volume down, as to not disturb Sinclair, until she saw something that caught her eye.

"I love these kids," Kate said, turning up the volume. "They have been in mass shootings and help other kids process the stress when it happens to them. I went to a demonstration against guns in D.C. and heard some of them speak. They are heartbreaking and so inspiring."

Kate knew that she felt a kinship with them because of what she'd experienced with Theo Mast. Luckily for her, she didn't have to live with the same trauma

"An eleven-year-old girl was shot eating a happy meal in Atlanta. Three were shot dead and three wounded at a Youngstown bar. A fourteen-year-old girl was shot at a concert in South Carolina. Three people were found shot to death in Atlanta.

Sixteen-year-old fatally shot and five wounded in Columbus. Nine-year-old shot while jumping on a trampoline. A woman was fatally shot while on a four-wheeler. A woman was shot by her child while driving on I-95 when her child found her gun in the backseat. A pregnant woman was shot while driving a car in Maryland. A six-year-old boy was shot dead while in a car during a road rage shooting. Three unarmed Black men were shot by the police in three different incidents on the same day. Eight mass shootings in the United States over the weekend, resulted in 24 dead and 42 wounded. This all happened during one week in America," the young man said, pausing to let it sink in.

I hate guns. Even before Theo Mast, I hated guns.

"On average, at least two Americans are shot accidentally by their dogs each year. We know, on average, 115,000 people are shot each year, with almost 39,000 dying from the bullets. Of those, 14,000 are murdered, 34,000 are intentionally shot by someone else and survive, 24,000 are suicides, and 550 are women shot by their husbands or partners. Around 1600 children and teens die from gunshots every year, while more than 6,000 are shot and survive," he continued while the panel and moderator stayed silent.

"Every day, 316 people are shot in the United States; on average, 106 of them die. These death numbers are not as high as the 3,000 dead from COVID-19 in a single day, but these gun deaths are every day, every year, for decades," he continued reading.

"Kate, can you turn that up?" Sinclair asked.

"We begged lawmakers to pass laws to make it stop. We pleaded with Americans to regain empathy and rational thinking and decide that their right to live, their loved ones' right to live, is more important than a couple of sentences written 250 years ago. Our values have changed since then. Everyone in America has the right to vote now. Our technology has changed since then; one gun can mow down dozens of people in seconds. We see everything because cameras are everywhere. We are wiping entire species into extinction, and we know we don't need these arsenals to hunt for food or protect ourselves from animals. We pleaded with America to stop the gun violence; half of America and most of the U.S. Senate decided to do nothing. They looked away from the heartbreak and misery and did nothing. Now, someone or something did, in just a few minutes, what our leaders would not: they stopped gun violence in America."

Wow, that's so insightful and true in a violent, twisted way. Rex was able to do what our most powerful people had failed to do.

A woman on the panel cut in and angrily asked the young man, "And you are happy about it? Happy that 70,000,000 Americans are dead?"

"No, of course, I'm not happy. I've been working to stop gun violence for years. Why would I be happy? That is a ridiculous accusation," he added.

The moderator walked in front of the camera. "No one is blaming anyone. We are just having a discussion. Some Americans are curious to know what proponents for gun regulations are thinking now, almost two months after the mass shooting."

A young lady leaned forward and said, "The hostility we have had directed at us from the President and others is crazy. If people had listened to us and put sane, responsible, strict gun rules and regulations in place, maybe fewer people would be dead today."

"That is ridiculous," the angry woman said. "If all your rules were in place, millions of law-abiding Americans would still be dead. Maybe people on the terrorist list, known spouse abusers, or those with a history of mental illness and violence would be alive because they could not own guns. They could have just walked out to the streets and picked up the discarded guns, making themselves the only armed Americans. Then, all of us who did not own a gun on July 14 could be victims."

A few people on the panel scoffed. The moderator dramatically scratched her head to show she was thinking through the logic.

A young teenager leaned forward and raised his hand.

"Go ahead, Archie. What would you like to contribute?" the moderator asked, encouraging him.

"Some of us have always said we hate guns. Guns kill kids. Guns kill kids in inner cities, like where I live and where my mom was shot and killed. Guns kill kids at school, church, movies, concerts, stores, and in cars. Guns are dangerous and bad, and July 14 is proof we should not have guns. I didn't see any good people with guns defending all those people. We need to get rid of guns once and for all," he said passionately.

Kate decided she would look up what happened to Theo Mast after the debate. She felt a strong desire to know if he died on July 14.

"I appreciate your thoughts and contributions, young man, but all those gun restrictions you and your friends wanted two months ago would not have stopped the mass shooting and could have made things worse!" the angry woman almost shouted.

The young man that read all the statistics cut in, "This is a pointless debate. Guns have killed hundreds of thousands of people over the past decades. Millions died on July 14 in just a few minutes. It was a mass suicide, so you can't blame anyone. If that mass shooting wasn't evidence that guns, not necessarily the gun owners, but guns, are bad, evil, dangerous then I don't know what is!"

"Exactly! You just made my point," the angry woman said.

The moderator jumped in and tried to clear things up. "So, Abby is saying guns don't kill people, people kill people. Archie and the anti-gun activists are saying that guns kill people. I am not sure what position is right," she said.

"No kidding. This debate is giving me a headache," Kate said to the TV.

"Who cares?" another young woman asked with disdain. "If there had been fewer guns in America on July 14, fewer people would be dead. That is a fact."

The angry woman started to cry. "I lost my husband, two sons, and my mother on July 14. They owned guns, exercising their second amendment rights, and they should be alive."

"So do the thousands killed in shootings before July 14! People that did not own guns also deserved to be alive!" the young woman snapped. "I am very sorry for your loss."

The angry woman, that now just seemed sad, wiped tears off her face and said, "Well, I am sure there is one thing we all agree on: Kate Stellute needs to be arrested. It needs to be determined exactly what she knew and when."

Kate sucked in her breath, stunned by the sudden change in direction of the conversation. There was a long silence. Neither the moderator nor any of the panelists said a word.

"Jesus," Sinclair said quietly.

Finally, the young man who had been reading off the statistics at the beginning said, "I'm curious to know what she knows. We really need to determine how and why this happened. Regardless of what she says, I still hope guns are a thing of the past and sanity prevails moving forward."

The moderator jumped in and said, "Well, it's good that we can end agreeing on one thing. We all want to hear from Kate Stellute."

Kate clicked off the TV, infuriated. "What the hell? So much incomprehensible death and destruction and pain to the human mind and heart, enormous global violence, and they actually think a 27-year-old analyst at Space Force did it? It blows my mind how stupid Americans can be!"

"Kate, ignore it. They are all scared and clinging to something irrational to make themselves feel better. Like they used to do with guns. What happened to the peace and love and good energy you were just sending into the universe?" Sinclair asked.

"I need more wine," Kate said, heading to the minifridge.

TWENTY-THREE

Fifty-One Days After the Shooting

Kate startled awake, another nightmare on the fringes of her memory. She was in a high-speed car chase on I-95 being followed by dozens of black SUVs, and she could not control the car. Sinclair kept screaming for her to slow down in the dream, making her feel more scared. She hated the feeling of being completely out of control.

Wait, was that a dream or my new reality?

"Ugh," Kate mumbled, rolling over and seeing Sinclair in the other bed.

Must have dozed off. Maybe we don't need two rooms.

Kate sat up and moved her toes along the dark floor to find her shoes.

Her head suddenly snapped toward the window; she heard a noise outside. Sinclair had pulled the curtains tightly closed. Even though it was very dark in the room, she could see a light gray crack along the top where the curtain didn't completely cover the glass.

It must be dawn already.

She put on her shoes and picked up her phone and room key, then she heard the noise again. This time, her heart started to pound. It sounded like a car door being shut.

"Sinclair, wake up," Kate whispered. "Someone's out there."

Sinclair did not stir. Kate leaned over and shook his shoulder.

"Jeez, Kate, you scared me," Sinclair said, rolling over.

"Sinclair, get up. Quietly. I think someone is outside. I heard noises," Kate whispered.

Sinclair shot straight up.

Kate put her finger to her lips, indicating to stay quiet. She moved to the window and slowly peeked through the curtain. She did not see anything suspicious. Sinclair startled her when he suddenly came up behind her.

Seeing nothing, Sinclair went back to the bed and put on his shoes, and picked up his phone.

"Let's just pack up and go. Hit the road now and be in Brevard by noon," Sinclair whispered.

Kate collected her few things, and whispered, "I need to go next door and get the rest of my stuff."

"Let's stick together; I'll go with you," Sinclair said as he picked up a bag with his toiletries, clothes, and chargers and put his laptops under his arm.

Kate opened the door slowly and stuck her head out a little to look right. She jumped when she saw several people standing there. She glanced left to see several more people. They were purposefully not standing in front of the door or window. Kate jumped back inside, pushed Sinclair aside, and slammed the door shut.

"What the hell?" Sinclair whispered loudly.

"They aren't Space Force. They aren't in uniform. They look like regular people," Kate whispered.

"Bam! Bam! Bam!" on the door startled them both.

"Kate Stellute, we know you are in there. We just saw you. Please come out. We need to talk to you," a man's voice called through the door.

Kate and Sinclair looked at each other but did not say a word.

"We need to ask you some questions about July 14. We have called the police," the voice said.

After another minute, the man shouted through the door, "We are going to come in. We have a key."

"The hell you are!" Sinclair called through the door. "We paid for this room. We deny you access. If you enter this room, you are breaking the law. Do not enter this room!"

Kate went into the bathroom and looked out the window, seeing more people.

When she returned to Sinclair's side, she whispered, "There are more in the back. I'm scared."

The door was opened with a key; when the inside lock engaged, someone kicked the door, breaking it. Kate and Sinclair jumped back away from it, almost tripping over a bed.

Several people barged through the broken door.

"We just want to ask you some questions," a middle-aged woman said with a snarl. "We just want to know how you did it. How you made the mass shooting happen? And tell us where Rex is! Just answer these questions, and you are free to go."

"You are not the police. Kate had nothing to do with the mass shooting. Please walk out of this room now, before things get more out of hand," Sinclair said calmly, trying to de-escalate the situation.

"We are not talking to you," the woman said to Sinclair.

"How did you find us?" Kate asked.

Did Claudia send them after us?

"That doesn't matter," a large, overweight man said, pushing his face into Kate's face. "Tell us how you did it! How you made our kids shoot themselves? Tell me how you got my dad, a proud decorated war veteran, to shoot himself!"

"I lost everyone!" the woman who spoke first shouted. "Everyone! Everyone I love! How did you do it? Why? Where is Rex?"

More people were walking into the small room, forcing Kate and Sinclair to back up.

"Maybe you should have some of your own medicine," another old man barked at them. "There are more ways to die than by a gun. My son would never have committed suicide. Never! He was happy and loved his job and family. You murdered him!"

"I had nothing to do with the mass shooting. I was running in a park near my house when it happened. I was as terrified and shocked as everyone. I learned about the guns and suicide watching the news, just like all of you. I was harassed by Rex in the park. I didn't cause the violence. I didn't know Rex before he harassed me, and I have no idea where he is. I would never hurt or kill anyone. I'm a vegan for God's sake. I have no idea how any of this happened!" Kate shouted loudly so everyone could hear. Her voice was shaking, and tears were filling her eyes.

"Step out of the room now or you will be arrested," a woman shouted just outside the motel room.

Kate and Sinclair put their hands up. They were up against the back wall. Too many people blocked their view of the door to know if it was more mob or cops.

"What the hell? Who in the hell are you?" the woman who first spoke asked, turning to shout out the door.

"You have to the count of ten to walk out of the room or you will be arrested," the woman called from outside.

"What the hell," the woman said again, pushing past the others and stomping out the door. "We have every right to find out what happened to our kids," she said, yelling at someone outside the door.

The room emptied quickly. It seemed that she was the leader as the rest followed her.

Sinclair and Kate stayed in the room.

"I am not eager to get arrested," Sinclair said, leaning against the wall with his hands still in the air.

Jo-Ellen walked into the room and said, "I guess we need to stay even closer together. I can't have some redneck mob kill our only connection to Rex. Get your stuff and let's get out of here."

Kate had never been so happy to see Space Force agents; up until now, they had only made her life more difficult.

Sinclair and Kate grabbed their things and walked out of the room. Kate decided to abandon her clothes and toiletries in the other room and rushed to Sinclair's car. Outside, Kate could see that the crowd was very large, and she feared the Space Force agents could lose control of it.

Kate could hear Tonya yelling at the crowd. Tonya was the lead investigator from Space Force and had seniority over Jo-Ellen. Kate had not seen Tonya since the interview at Space Force Headquarters.

"If you want to find out what happened, this is not helpful. You can't scare or harass citizens. As far as we know, they have not broken any laws. Making us come here is just distracting us from our important work. We all want to know what happened. We are also suspicious and watching Kate Stellute, but we need to work together. You, the concerned public, and us, the government, have to work together," Tonya explained loudly so the crowd could hear her.

"Are they throwing us under the bus again?" Kate asked Sinclair as she got in the car. "Is Tonya telling them they need to work together against us?"

"That's how it sounds," Sinclair responded, driving quickly out of the parking lot, and heading south.

TWENTY-FOUR

Fifty-One Days After the Shooting

They drove in silence for a while. Kate did not want to hear music or the news. She glanced at Sinclair; he looked angry and tired. She was overwhelmed by the desire to be at home with Kyle. She was tired of the constant fear, tension, and anxiety.

I want this nightmare over.

"We get to Brevard, and we find the debris. We determine if it's a viable clue that will help us with Rex and help stop more violence. We stay focused and on the mission," Sinclair said.

Kate looked at him. *Is he reading my mind?* She nodded in agreement.

"How did the mob find us? I know Space Force follows us," Kate said. "Fast food drive-thru, quick stops at gas stations, and I didn't even go into the hotel reception. I haven't since the first night. People can't recognize me with the mask, hat, and sunglasses, and they don't know who you are. You haven't been in the news. Well, not yet. It does not make any sense. Who tipped off that huge mob? Where did they come from?"

She was talking fast like she was scared or still running on adrenalin.

"Must be the car," Sinclair said. "I'm probably on the internet in the nutbag, right-wing conspiracy world by now. What is left of those sites and those people, anyway; I assume many of them owned guns." Sinclair took a deep breath and continued, "I could be stereotyping. Maybe they are just regular Americans in a lot of pain. I don't know. I don't look at those sites, so I have no idea what is being said or how they found us."

Sinclair sounded agitated and frustrated, his hands gripping the steering wheel.

"Jo-Ellen or anyone at Space Force could have leaked that we are together. Maybe shown a picture of you and the car on social media," Kate continued speculating, still feeling hyped-up. "They are probably setting us up to take the blame when the next round of violence happens. We're the scapegoats, and I'm sorry I dragged you into this!"

"Kate, you didn't drag me into anything. I wouldn't be here if I didn't feel passionate about understanding Rex and solving the puzzle; I care about you and want to help. I have a lot of reasons to be here with you," Sinclair said, briefly looking at Kate.

"You know, back when I was being questioned at Space Force, Jo-Ellen called me brave. I wasn't exactly sure what she was referencing; I felt like she was feeding my ego or something. It's obnoxious how we are taught that honesty and bravery are admirable traits that should be respected, yet no one wants real honesty or real bravery. They want scared lemmings to control. I'm supposedly brave, but in my experience, no one listens to me, and they're quick to throw me under the bus when I tell the truth," Kate said.

"Tell me about it," Sinclair said, keeping his eyes on the rearview mirror. "In my field, we use complex evidence-based science to research the possibility of extraterrestrial life on other planets, but most of my research must be done under the radar. For example, looking for signs of life on Mars is acceptable. Our government thought finding some simple, carbon-based evidence of life on other planets would be good; it would help make the case to explore space and spend billions of dollars to get more people out there to explore, extract, and dominate. It's also self-centered; some think if we find any life on other planets, humans can exist there as well."

Kate was riveted. Sinclair had never talked about his work so much.

"However, even though there have been legitimate UFOs and UAPs sightings here since the 1960s, and numerous distinguished scientists like Carl Sagan, James McDonald, and Allen Hynek think they should be investigated, it's considered fringe science at best. I can't tell the public or Congress about some of my research because they think it's a joke. 'The powers that be' decided an advanced extraterrestrial can't come here, to Earth, and so it's truth."

Sinclair got quiet, and his eyes lingered on the rearview mirror causing Kate to look out the back window. A vehicle was approaching quickly. When it flew past them at a dangerous speed, they smiled at each other with relief.

Sinclair continued, "Finding carbon-based materials or any evidence of advanced life here from somewhere else is not supported. It might scare the public. It doesn't fit the narrative that has been created and controlled for decades."

"Who created the narrative?" Kate asked.

"NASA, DOD, the government, and academia supports them because they are often their funding sources. I don't think it was intended to hurt anyone; it's just a self-centered, safe, and lazy way to think. That's all changed now because of Rex," Sinclair said.

"What exactly do you mean?" Kate asked.

"Well, Rex has proven there is advanced life out there, and the government can't deny that now. Rex has also changed the narrative. Rex might have provided justifications for creating Space Force and weaponizing space, which is good for military contractors and the politicians they own. Legitimate open and transparent scientific research would have furthered our knowledge and potentially prevented Rex's anger and the mass shooting in the first place," Sinclair said. "The government can do all kinds of things in the name of making us safe but fails constantly."

"But what makes us safe? It's not guns and weapons anymore if they ever did," Kate said, looking at Sinclair. "So, were you brave and honest for suspecting there was advanced life out there? Or are you crazy and fringe? We should let facts and science decide, not politicians. Politicians base their decisions on how it helps their personal goals, elections, donations, and corporate profits. It's always about money."

Sinclair shook his head in agreement. "Like that kid, Theo Mast. I bet he had wealthy parents, right?"

"You got it," Kate said, remembering the slick lawyer his family hired to redirect the blame on her. Her mother, on her elementary school teacher budget, could not hire an attorney. Instead, they had to move.

Kate noticed that Sinclair was driving ten miles below the speed limit. She said, "Hey, can you pick it up? I'm getting tired of being in this car."

"Sorry," he said, accelerating but not breaking the 65mph restriction. "I try not to give cops any reason to pull me over."

"Okay, you'll help a possible fugitive escape menacing black SUVs and the feds, but you won't drive 70?" Kate teased, but her effort at levity fell flat. Sinclair's knuckles were still white, his hands tightly gripping the steering wheel.

"Our society is fucked up. Lemmings and cowards everywhere. Most people don't want to rock the boat for anyone or anything. Look at the world we are living in now," Sinclair said. "Sorry for the rant; I'm just furious about that mob. The audacity of storming into our room and threatening us. It's messing with my head."

Kate took Sinclair's hand and pulled it to her face. He smelled like a combination of hand sanitizer and salt, with a little sweat from his death grip on the wheel. It was comforting.

"You can vent to me anytime you want; your feelings are completely valid."

Sinclair pulled his hand back, reached for his phone, and dialed a number.

"I have an idea," he said, putting the call on speaker.

A woman with a loud voice answered. "Hi, Sinclair! How are you?"

"Hi, Karisma! I'm okay. I'll be in your neighborhood around noon, and I need your help," he replied.

Karisma? Another colleague of Yvette's? Someone else to suck into this dangerous drama?

"What? You're in Florida? Why? Oh, never mind, tell me when you get here. Come and stay at one of my places."

"Actually, I need your help as soon as we get there. I need to hide my car and borrow another for a few days. I would love to stay at one of your properties, if possible, without a paper trail. Can you help me out?" he asked.

"Hmmm. Intriguing. You know I'd do anything for you. You're in luck; most of my vacation rentals are empty. This whole town is empty. Let me round up a set of keys and address and call you back. Can't wait to hear what you are up to. Can't wait to do a proper toast to my baby sister," the woman replied.

Baby sister? Is she Yvette's sister?

"And Larry. Okay, I will call you when I'm an hour out. Thanks, Karisma," Sinclair said and hung up. "Oh shit, here they come." His eyes drifted to the rearview mirror.

"Who?" Kate asked, looking over her shoulder and seeing several black SUVs on the road behind them.

"Our escort to Brevard County," Sinclair replied.

TWENTY-FIVE

Fifty-One Days After the Shooting

As they got off the highway and headed east, Kate could immediately see the impact the shooting had on Florida. I-95 had been pretty empty since they left D.C., but it felt like a Sunday morning or just a lucky time with no traffic. But there should have been way more traffic in a city in Florida at noon on a Thursday, even during a pandemic. Cars were so rare that their movement caught her eye.

"It looks and feels like this town is about to be hit by a level five hurricane," Kate said.

"Exactly. Given we don't have traffic to hide in, I don't know how we're going to lose our sinister Space Force friends," Sinclair said. "We're like ten minutes away from where we need to meet Karisma. With no traffic, they can just follow along."

Sinclair's phone made a noise, and Kate picked it up and read the text.

"Karisma sent an address and gate code. We must be going to a gated community," Kate said. "That's cool; maybe if we pull in fast, we can block them there at the gate and make it a little harder on them."

Sinclair drove through different neighborhoods with the three cars still on their tail. "I know this area well. I think I'll meander around and see if we can lose them."

As they drove through cute, colorful neighborhoods, Kate looked for people, but she did not see a single one.

"Well, there were five, but now they're down two. Either they're trying to head us off or they have another plan. Maybe we can lose another one heading beachside," Kate said. "Maybe someone may have to pee like a racehorse, and they will head to a hotel."

The two SUVs followed them over the bridge to the barrier island. The light was turning red when Sinclair made a fast, sharp left, leaving the other two vehicles behind.

"They didn't make the light!" Kate said, her heart beating. Sinclair quickly turned again onto a small road leading to a community with a double gate and guard station.

"Code?" Sinclair asked. "Quick. They can just run that light."

Kate read it fast, Sinclair pressed the buttons quickly, and they both held their breath as they waited for the gate to lift.

"They aren't behind us yet," Sinclair said as he sped through the gate, squealing around a bend to get out of eyeshot.

"Careful, Sinclair. We don't want to hit a dog or a squirrel or child!" Kate said, looking behind her.

"Address? This is a fancy community; the condos have closed garages which is helpful. I told Karisma we needed to hide the car," Sinclair said.

"There it is!" Kate said, excited to find it so fast.

The garage door lifted slowly, and Sinclair drove inside. The door closed behind them, and they sat quietly in the dark garage for a moment. A woman came through a side door and called to them. "Sinclair? Is that you?"

"Yes," Sinclair said, getting out of the car. "Is that you Angelina? It has been a while, but I remember that face."

"Whoops, you shouldn't. Let me put this damn thing on," she said, putting a mask on. "I have no idea what's going on. I manage these properties. Karisma called and asked me to keep a car in a closed garage here for a week or so. I was hesitant at first, but then she told me it was for you and that you are in some kind of situation. Of course, I will help you!" she said, opening her arms wide to hug Sinclair. "Okay, grab your stuff; we have to go," she said, abruptly pulling out of the hug.

Kate put on her disguise and grabbed her few belongings. Sinclair opened the backseat door and pulled out his computers and files. They followed Angelina through some very tidy, flowerbox-lined paths that ran between the buildings and into another garage, where they found a rundown service van. The side door was open, and Kate and Sinclair crawled in.

"This is my son, Anton. He'll drive you to Karisma's. Wait, Sinclair, is that car yours or stolen?" Angelina asked as she was about to slide the van door shut.

"What? It's mine. Not stolen, I assure you," Sinclair said, seeming surprised by the question.

"Okay, give me the keys. I might have to drive it to another spot, and I don't trust the police around here, with or without guns," she said as she closed the door.

Sinclair and Kate focused on not sliding around too much or damaging their equipment on the twenty-minute drive. There were no windows in the back of the van, and it was hot. When the van stopped, they were eager to get out. They were in another dark garage.

"Anton, thanks for the ride. We really appreciate it," Sinclair said as they climbed out.

Anton was very tall and thin; Kate thought he looked to be around twenty.

"Sure, no problem," he said. He was wearing a mask that read "I can't breathe."

"Did you see any black SUVs following us? Maybe near the gate when you pulled out of the community where you picked us up? Sinclair asked.

"No, and I think I would have noticed. I go in there a lot with this van, doing work for my mom. You'll in trouble?" Anton asked, sounding curious, but not worried.

"Sort of. It's just a mistake we need to clear up. Nothing to worry about. You won't get in any trouble. We promise you that," Sinclair said.

Suddenly, the door to the house opened and a gorgeous woman rushed through, arms opened wide for

Sinclair. She looked like an older version of Yvette, but far flashier with fancy clothes, heels, braids, and fingernails.

"It's so good to see you, Sinclair!" she squealed. They hugged for a full minute.

Kate waited patiently beside the van. She knew this was one of those mourning hugs. When they broke apart, they both had tears in their eyes.

"It's sweltering in here. Let's get inside to the AC. Come on," Karisma said, picking up a computer to help as she led the way into the house. "Anton, come in for a drink before you dehydrate, baby."

The house was nice; it had that short-term rental house feel, clean with nice decorations, but no real personality.

"Two bedrooms and a bathroom on that side of the house," Karisma said, pointing. Master bedroom and bathroom on this side. Take your pick. The kitchen is fully loaded with cooking equipment, and there's good Wi-Fi, way better than a hotel. It's three miles to the beach, so you better drive because it is hot, hot, hot. A couple of miles to my bar. I put some drinks and snacks in the fridge. All the details and rules are on the fridge, but you are my guests, of course, so ignore all that fee stuff. What is your name again, baby?"

"Kate. Thanks for letting us stay, and for helping hide Sinclair's car," Kate replied.

"No problem. Though I am curious about what's going on. Let me get some drinks," Karisma said, heading into the kitchen.

Kate went to the bathroom in the master bedroom and splashed cold water on her face, trying to freshen up the best she could without her basic hygiene products. Then, she looked around, opening drawers and cupboards and finding many unopened supplies, including a toothbrush and toothpaste. There was even shampoo in the shower and a hair dryer. Kate decided to take a shower to give Sinclair and Karisma some private time to catch up.

She felt a million times better once she was clean. She had run out of the motel that morning without even brushing her teeth. After a ten-minute power nap wrapped in a towel, she dried her hair, and with great sadness, put on her sweaty and dirty bra, t-shirt, and shorts. Even with the old clothes, she felt dramatically better than when she entered the house.

She put on a crumpled mask with a cheerful rainbow and went into the living room where she found Karisma and Sinclair drinking beers, their feet propped up on the coffee table.

"Grab a beer and join us," Sinclair said.

Beer made her think of Kyle; they would sit on their front porch, him with a beer and her with a jumbo glass of Pinot Noir. *I need to check in with him soon.*

Kate stood in front of the fridge, checking out the tourist-friendly magnets of manatees and palm trees. Then she grabbed a beer, went back into the living room, and plopped down on a chair near Sinclair. "The shower felt great. Thank you, Karisma."

Karisma flashed a smile that reminded her of Yvette. "Sure. This is your place for as long as you need it. Sinclair was catching me up. He told me ya'll are here to track down some of Yvette's work. That it might be related to the shooting? Have to admit, it sounds crazy to me. He explained that you helped him when he needed help with Yvette on July 14, and for that, I am very grateful to you," Karisma said, taking a swig of beer. "One thing he left out is why he is working with you, Kate Stellute, the only person of interest in the mass shooting."

Sinclair choked on his beer. Kate realized he was only telling Karisma half the story. She was stunned to be recognized; she was careful to keep a mask on and her hair up.

"Girl, you're all they talk about on FOX news. This county has pretty much decided you did it. Or you and this mysterious Rex guy were in cahoots. I doubt a person around here would not recognize you, even in a cute mask. Many of the redneck, racist dumbasses died on July 14, so you're safe from them, but many of their loved ones are alive and well. They're scared and angry and looking for someone to blame. I must admit, when I first saw you on the news and all the stories about you online, I was hoping it was your fault. I guess so it was not my Larry's fault. I miss him so much," Karisma paused, slowly finishing her beer.

"I'm sorry for your loss," Kate said, feeling the hollowness of the words. "I'm a very peaceful person. I hate guns. I hate violence. I won't even eat animals." Kate tried to defend herself. Now two people Sinclair trusted had negative impressions of her.

I hope they don't think less of him for working with me.

"You don't have to tell me twice, sweetie. If Sinclair trusts you, then I trust you too. Anyway, I hate to leave you, but I have to get to work. I only have one place open now. Half my staff died in the shooting. Half my regulars are dead. A skeleton crew is what's left, mostly employees that have been with me for years. I stay open to provide some community and friendship in these bleak times. We're always running out of food, beer, and drinks, but people are patient. It's like after a really bad storm: we're all in this together. Come by later for dinner, and I can whip up some fresh fish. Stay safe," Karisma called over her shoulder as she walked out the front door.

Sinclair and Kate finished their beers in silence.

"We came for a reason, a purpose. Let's go find those materials and see what they tell us," Kate said.

"Are you sure? I can go alone. It might be safer for you to stay here," Sinclair said.

Kate didn't feel safe though. She half-expected Jo-Ellen to walk through the front door, and she didn't want Sinclair to do this next part alone. "I don't want us to split up. I feel safer when we're together. Do we have a car?" Kate asked.

"Yes. Anton got a car from someone; it might be one of Karisma's or Larry's? I am not exactly sure, but it's in the garage for our use. Are you sure, Kate?" Sinclair asked again.

"Very sure. Let's go," Kate said.

TWENTY-SIX

Fifty-One Days After the Shooting

In the car, a white CR-V, Sinclair was talking about what Kate had been thinking earlier. "I hate putting on these dirty clothes. We need to go to a store," Sinclair said. "In the movies, people don't seem to mind wearing the same clothes for days, but I feel gross. I'm not cut out for the secret-agent-UFO-chasing life."

"We sound like Jo-Ellen; she hates being a field agent. Besides, those movies aren't usually in Florida where it's so hot," Kate said, nodding in agreement.

Sinclair called Claudia. Kate's knees bobbed up and down with nerves. She knew that Claudia didn't like or trust her. Sinclair put the call on speaker.

"Is Kate Stellute still with you?" Claudia asked right away.

"Yes, sorry I didn't tell you," Sinclair said into the phone while looking at Kate. "I know you know; you're very smart. Listen, Claudia, she had absolutely nothing to do with July 14; I promise you. We are working together to find out what happened. Please know, with all confidence, that you are helping the good guys," Sinclair said.

Claudia was quiet for a moment. "Start at Kennedy Space Center. I heard the majority of KSC security staff died in the mass shooting, so your and Yvette's badges might get you in. Be upfront and say you work for NASA, as did Yvette, and you want to collect her personal belongings," Claudia said.

"Yes. I will try. I do want to get to her desk if possible. And I do work for NASA, and I have my badge; we are all on the same team. Thanks, Claudia," Sinclair said.

"I don't know what you are doing. I know what I see on the news. I don't think you should trust her, Sinclair, and honestly, I don't understand any of it. The more I think about it, I just can't logically figure out how she could have caused it. I don't understand how Rex could do it either. Reluctantly, I have no choice but to support whatever you are doing for Yvette or for Jack or NASA," Claudia said, sounding defeated.

"I assure you, Claudia, Kate is a good person. You can call NASA, Space Force, or anyone you want to tell them what we've discussed; we don't want to get you into any trouble. Wait, have you already spoken to them? We had a little trouble on the road," Sinclair said.

"I seriously considered it, but I didn't call any authorities. Honestly, my curiosity about the collision and Yvette's research trumped my suspicion of Kate's involvement in the shooting. I am a scientist after all. Plus, she is on the news everywhere; America suspects her, and Americans are looking for her. I'm sure Space Force and NASA are tracking you two; hell, the CIA, FBI, and DOD are probably in on it too. They don't need a call from me. Let me know what you find. Stay safe, Sinclair," Claudia said before hanging up.

Before Kate could ask Sinclair if he believed Claudia, Sinclair dialed another number and put the call on speaker.

"Sinclair, my friend, how are you? Are we still set to meet Friday morning?" Jack asked.

"Not unless you're in Brevard County, Florida," Sinclair responded.

"No. Wait, dude, I thought we were meeting in Houston. What happened? Why are you in Florida?" Jack asked, sounding disappointed.

"I need to get into Kennedy to access Yvette's office and files. My badge may work, but I might need backup. Any ideas?" Sinclair winked at Kate.

"It's closed to the public because of COVID. Most of the security detail died in the shooting. There's very little staff working, so once you get through the gate, you should have free range. I beefed up my private detail there because I feared security breaches; everything is totally fucked. I can't let that Boston asshat, or the others, near my research; they all steal and cheat. I hired a team from Patrick Air Force Base, or should I say Patrick Space Force Base and Cape Canaveral Space Force Base," Jack laughed loudly, speaking incoherently for a moment. "I'm sure they have nothing better to do!"

Is he drunk again?

Kate took a moment to text her mom and Kyle to let them know that she was healthy and safe. She would call them later. She made sure to tell them that she loved them, just in case something went wrong.

TWENTY-SEVEN

Fifty-One Days After the Shooting

To calm her nerves, Kate counted CR-Vs as they drove. The few times they saw other cars, it was almost always a white CR-V. On the forty-minute drive to Kennedy Space Center, Kate counted five white CR-Vs. "Sinclair, I honestly think CR-Vs are the official car of Florida. My mom drives one, too. It's strange," she mused.

Sinclair nodded and replied, "Florida."

As they turned on the road leading into Kennedy Space Center, Kate's nerves spiked.

What if Sinclair's badge doesn't work? What if the guard doesn't buy his story about cleaning out Yvette's belongings? What if my image is plastered on the bulletin board in their break room with a "WANTED" poster in big bold letters?

"What's the plan?" Kate asked. "How will we get in? Are we going to drive into the complex and hope for the best? Oh, number six," Kate said as another CR-V came toward them from the other direction.

Sinclair slowed to a stop as the other CR-V pulled over, a five-foot grassy medium separated them. The driver wore army fatigues and shouted out the window, "It's all closed. The Space Center, offices; nothing is open, and no one is allowed in except for essential personnel."

"Gotcha, thanks," Sinclair called back. "I work for NASA. I need to get in on a special detail."

Just as Sinclair started to close the window and drive to the gate, the soldier yelled, "Wait, are you Sinclair Jones?"

"Yes," Sinclair replied.

"I will circle around and lead you in. Jack sent me," the soldier responded.

Sinclair and Kate waited as the soldier drove around and in front of their car. He pulled up to the security gate first, speaking to the guards for a couple of minutes before driving through. Sinclair pulled up, and the guard asked for his NASA identification.

Kate looked down, hoping they wouldn't ask for her ID. She didn't have identification of any kind since she had to run for her life when she left her house.

Jeez, was that just three days ago?

"Here you go, Dr. Jones," the guard said, handing the ID back. "I was told you worked here for several years, but since you're not currently assigned to this location, I must insist you stay with Lieutenant Kimmins at all times. We have cameras everywhere and will know if you separate."

"Got it. No problem," Sinclair responded.

"Well played, Jack," Sinclair said as they pulled away from the guard station.

"Seriously. I thought he was too drunk to understand what you were saying about changing destinations," Kate said.

"We're heading to hangar ten, way at the end. If my reading of the coordinates is correct, that is where the majority of debris will be. I don't care where Lieutenant Kimmins is going. It seems like he is heading to the offices, which makes sense because I told Jack I wanted to check Yvette's files," Sinclair said.

From what Kate could see, Kimmins was heading to the storied Kennedy Center Headquarters; she could see the famous NASA symbol and the American flag. "It still gives me goosebumps," Kate said. "It has since I was a teenager and first came here on a school tour. I haven't been in that building for years. I came here my first year at NASA to attend a training conference for new staff. I was so proud, walking in as an employee of NASA. Maybe we should go in there first? Find Yvette's office? Act like that's the main reason we are here? Go to the hangar later."

Sinclair shook his head and drove past the building. "Time is of the essence. We have to prioritize. A pack of Space Force SUVs could descend upon us at any moment. They must know we are here or are headed here. Let's get straight to hangar ten," he said.

"I forgot how huge this compound is," Kate said as they drove along for several minutes.

"This road of retired launch pads is like the history of America post WWII. See, those are the most primitive pads from the 1950s," Sinclair said, pointing toward the beach. "Back then, people could just hunker down behind sandbags and watch the launches. The launches were secure from Russian spies by Patrick and Cape Canaveral, but the public could get close. Each launch pad grew bigger, more complicated, and more powerful until we sent humans to the moon and beyond. It is amazing and awe-inspiring."

"I came on a tour with a Natural Resource Manager when I was here for training. I was just as interested in the ecosystem and wildlife as the launch pads. He told me how they manage endangered species on the property; he and his staff literally move some animals out of harm's way for launches. They would climb trees, capture them, or shoo them away to safety. He must be really busy now with so many more launches. Oh, look! A Florida scrub jay!" Kate said with excitement, pointing at a bird. "That's an endangered species."

"Cool," Sinclair said, squinting in the direction that Kate was pointing.

"The Natural Resource Manager also explained how important the environment was to choosing this location, with the lagoon on one side and the Atlantic Ocean on the other. It's so the burning components can fall and be extinguished. We also came upon a huge dead alligator on one of the roads. He said a garbage truck heading to a hangar had hit it. I asked how they could not have seen it since the gator was huge and no one drives very fast on a compound. He just shrugged, and told me that some people enjoy killing animals," Kate said, watching the pads go by as they drove.

"It is part of America's unique history," Sinclair said. "All this extraordinary natural beauty and extraordinary technology together."

"He also said we will lose them soon, the early pads, at least through the 1970s," Kate said with a sigh.

"Why?" Sinclair asked. "How?"

"Climate change. He said sea level rise would swallow them into the ocean. I told him that there was no way NASA and the government would let that happen, and he looked at me like I was stupid or naïve. Clearly, he was right. No one cares enough about the environment or nature to stop their destructive behavior. Not individuals, not the government, not even NASA, which employs the smartest people in the world. It's so sad," Kate said.

"I think this is the hangar. I hope we can get in. Where is Kimmins? I thought for sure he would turn around and follow us," Sinclair said, head pivoting side to side to look through the windows. "Something's not right; this is too easy."

"Should we forget it?" Kate asked, her own heart taking up residence in her throat. The huge parking lot was empty, and they had not seen another car or person in some time; it was unsettling.

"Hell no," Sinclair said. "Given the way our government is ignoring Rex, they are clearly hell-bent on self-destruction. It's on us to find out why Rex came and caused the mass shooting. I don't want to lose another 70,000,000 Americans. Let's find out what's in there. Okay?"

"We came this far," Kate said, eyeing the ominous hangar.

TWENTY-EIGHT

Fifty-One Days After the Shooting

"Now this really seems like a scene out of a post-apocalyptic movie. Like every human on Earth is dead, and we are the only remaining survivors," Kate whispered as they approached the front door.

"Then why are you whispering?" Sinclair asked in a loud whisper, smiling.

Kate rattled the front door, but it was locked. They started to walk around the building, trying every door and window they found. When they were in the back of the building, they found one unlocked.

"This is just too easy," Sinclair said, holding it open for Kate. "Either there is nothing in here and Jack, Space Force, and NASA are just letting us play around with our quest, or they want us in here finding something."

"Or it's a trap," Kate said, grateful she'd sent Kyle and her mom loving texts earlier.

It was dark in the huge windowless hangar. They moved along the walls, sometimes using their phones to see as they looked for a light switch.

"The air conditioner is on. People must be working in here sometimes," Sinclair said.

"Move along the wall until we get near the front door; there has to be a light switch near the front door," Kate said.

"Found something!" Sinclair said excitedly.

As the lights illuminated the vast space, they saw pieces of equipment spread on the floor throughout. The pieces were of various sizes; some pieces were huge, others medium, or very small. They walked toward the closet piece.

"Object #657, Jackson, Mississippi, retrieved, September 11, 2019," Kate read off the card on the floor. "Object #45, Galveston Bay, retrieved July 3, 2019. Object #211, Pascagoula, Mississippi, retrieved July 9, 2019. Object #301, Gulf of Mexico, retrieved June 30, 2019," Kate continued to read aloud as she moved slowly among the objects.

Sinclair was studying each object carefully. Kate wandered from one to the other, giving him space.

After some time had passed, Kate moved closer to him and watched him study and touch the objects. Some had extensive notes, in addition to the identification card, that he would slowly read.

If this room full of bent metal is our best hope to exonerate me and save the world, we're screwed.

"Okay Sinclair, what are your initial thoughts?" Kate asked, breaking the silence. They had been in the hangar for over an hour. She couldn't figure out what any of this debris had to do with Rex and his threats or how finding it would stop future violence.

"Some of it looks like it's ours, meaning made on Earth, not necessarily NASA's. But most of it is strange. The records indicate scientists and engineers are taking guesses, using deductive reasoning and the process of elimination to figure it out. I would say that some of these materials, minerals, and elements are not from here. We were right to think that there was a huge collision last year; it could have been something man-made with something otherworldly, and Rex is angry about it. So angry that he killed hundreds of millions of humans by simply turning our own technology on us," Sinclair said. "I'm a little pissed that I wasn't told about this, given my expertise. Neither NASA nor Yvette let me in on this amazing discovery."

Anger rose from Kate's feet to the top of her head. "But then they should know what Rex was talking about all along!"

She took a few deep, calming breaths and continued. "What sort of security clearance would one need to be in on all of this?" Kate asked, spreading her arms wide.

"Oh, the highest level, definitely need-to-know. They may even have kept all this from the president," Sinclair said.

"Well, given his big mouth, that would be smart," Kate said. "I think you're right; they let us find this. I know everyone is short-staffed but zero security? No real escort. The question is: Why? Why do they want us here?" Kate sighed, looking to the door, expecting Jo-Ellen to barge in at any moment. "Do you think

Jack knew this was here? I mean, he sounded very eager to learn what Yvette knew about the collision. If this has been here for days, weeks, months, then he must have known. No wonder Kimmins just let us go on our merry way," Kate said.

"I don't understand why this would be unguarded. None of this makes any sense," Sinclair said, scratching his head.

They spent another couple of hours studying, reading, and taking pictures of objects and their identifying information.

"Like what the hell is this?" Kate asked, laughing as she picked up an object, seemingly made from rainbow plastic; it looked more like a children's toy than high-tech from outer space.

Kate had stopped checking the door every few minutes, satisfied the feds weren't coming after all.

"This is really cool. Absolutely amazing. It proves without a doubt that an advanced life form exists in the galaxy. I'm so happy I got to see this. It's confirmation of my life's work, even if I was not included; I was not wrong, and it's evidence that everything has a price," Sinclair said.

"It really is extraordinary. But now, Sinclair, I am going to be extremely ordinary; I'm starving, and I want a clean shirt. Let's go," Kate said, taking his hand.

They turned off the lights and walked out the same back door they came in. They walked along the side of the building, heading to the front where they had parked Karisma's CR-V.

"You know, we can come back tomorrow; no one seems to care we are here. So why not?" Kate asked.

As they turned the bend, they both gasped. Sinclair dropped her hand, raising both of his arms into the air.

A ring of at least twenty black SUVs surrounded the front of the warehouse. Several of the acting generals from Space Force and Jo-Ellen, Tonya, Malcolm, and the other guy were all standing near the SUVs. Kimmins and Jack were next to a flashy sportscar. There were a few assault weapon vehicles that looked like tanks and several police cars.

Tanks? This might really be the end!

Kate wished she had one more chance to hear her mother's voice and to say goodbye to Kyle. She reached for Sinclair's hand again, pulling it down to her side, and whispered, "Guess the hangar is soundproof as well as air-conditioned. Should we make a run for it?"

Sinclair choked back a small laugh and squeezed her hand.

"Seriously, everyone needs to stand down!" Kate shouted so everyone could hear.

They wouldn't shoot us in broad daylight, right? If that was their intent, they would have done it already. It's not like we led them to this massive secret; most of these people must know what's in this hangar.

"We saw the evidence of a collision. Now Rex's anger makes sense. We know there is an enormous amount of dangerous pollution in space, and he wants it cleaned up. No one has learned anything new today. Well, except that we saw some very cool stuff which confirmed our thinking." Kate started coughing, "It's not COVID; I'm dehydrated and in need of water and a bullhorn!"

Sinclair started to laugh and said, "You're crazy, Kate."

The Acting General of Space Force approached them and said, "I find it interesting that you are enjoying this. Feel it's worthy of jokes. I guess you think 70,000,000 dead Americans is a joke. Put your hands up; you're under arrest. We've had enough of this."

"Enough of what? Honesty? Curiosity? What are we under arrest for? You let us drive in here. Guided us even and left the door unlocked. You provided proof that there was a massive collision, most likely caused by space debris. We know that the pollution in space triggered the mass shooting. It's all of *you* that should be arrested!" Kate shouted to the crowd.

A few police started to approach them, and Sinclair put his hands in the air, lifting Kate's too.

"What crime did we commit?" Kate demanded as she stepped back, pulling Sinclair with her.

"Never mind all that," a very old police officer said. "You're going with Space Force, lady, and your boy is coming with us. We don't need guns to enforce the law here."

Kate's blood ran cold as the cops pulled out tasers. She was terrified for Sinclair and felt a huge wave of guilt for getting him in this mess. She looked at the wall of mostly white power casually standing in front of them.

"Wait," Kate yelled so everyone could hear, not just the police approaching them. "What do you want?"

"Rex!" yelled two of the uniformed Space Force employees. Kate recognized them from the conference room.

"I can't give you Rex; I don't have him. Rex told me to deliver a message. I did. You chose to ignore that message. I have no idea how to reach him. So how can I give him to you?" Kate yelled so angrily and loudly that she coughed again.

She took a few slow steps backward, squeezing Sinclair's raised hand and pulling him along with her.

"I feel a strong urge to run, Sinclair. They will hurt you to hurt me. I don't trust any of them. They're cruel and self-centered and greedy," Kate said, turning her head toward him and looking him straight in the eye as she continued to pull them both slowly backward. "They're monsters. They're liars. They don't have guns. We can't let those tasers get any closer. We have to run; we're fit and can outrun them."

Kate thought of all those runs she used to happily take in the days before Rex; she could run an eight-minute mile with no problem.

"They don't have guns, but they do have tanks, fast cars, and definitely fists," Sinclair said, pulling her against him as they continued to walk slowly backward.

"There is no way in hell you are going anywhere with these people," Kate said, grabbing his hand and pulling him behind the building.

The cops chased after them, but Kate and Sinclair, even tired and dehydrated, were in far better shape. Kate willed her feet to go faster as she dragged Sinclair across the parking lot toward the surrounding woods.

"We will find you in a heartbeat; it's hot and there are so many mosquitoes. Come back and let's talk," Jo-Ellen's voice bellowed through a bullhorn.

"I knew they had a bullhorn!" Kate yelled to Sinclair as they ran. "Head toward the water; we can lose these assholes in the mangroves!"

The ground started to shake, and before she knew it, Kate was flying at a speed that brought her stomach into her mouth. She tried to scream but couldn't.

She opened her eyes in the white room as she hit the floor, gagging and gasping on all fours. She put her head down, and as soon as she had enough air, croaked, "No, Rex! They will kill him! You have to put me back!" Kate coughed and cried through chattering teeth. "Please put me back!"

For a minute, she sat cross-legged on the floor with her head down, trying to quickly regain equilibrium. She was shivering and wrapped her arms around her knees for warmth. In seconds, it went from 90 degrees to freezing.

After another minute, she could breathe without gasping or gagging. A couple of minutes after that, she could feel the room warm, and she stopped shivering. The second she was able, she stood up, looking at Rex as he sat across the room.

"Rex, please, Sinclair is in danger. They can kill him right now for no reason. I know that might not make sense to you, but I have to stop it. Please, please, please put me back," Kate begged.

"Sinclair is safe," Rex said slowly.

"You don't understand; they don't need guns or a reason. They'll kill him because he's in their way or seen as a nuisance. He is a Black man; they won't care that he has no criminal record and is a top astrophysicist. They will find an excuse to destroy him, probably with lots of pain, just because he helped me. They blame me for the shooting you caused! Please send me back now!" Kate pleaded, tears streaming down her face.

"Sinclair is here," Rex said in his very slow elocution.

Kate looked around the room, finding him way off to her left. He was squirming on the floor, gasping for breath, and shivering. Kate rushed to him and stroked his head. "Calm, Sinclair, be calm. Small, calm breaths. Don't panic. The air is here; it was stopped on the way here, but now there is air. Just calm, small breaths," she soothed. Kate rubbed his arms, face, and hands to warm him. She knew the sudden painful cold was terrifying. "Feel how it's warming up. You will be okay. You're safe. Just breathe," Kate said calmly, over and over.

TWENTY-NINE

Fifty-One Days After the Shooting

"**W**hat happened? Where are we?" Sinclair asked through chattering teeth.

"We are okay. You are okay. Just breathe," Kate said, massaging his back and arms. "You were curious about Rex; now you get to meet him. Ask him all your questions. And you're not getting tasered by toxic cops. Everything is okay."

For the first time since their first encounter, Kate was grateful for Rex. She was relieved that Sinclair was safe.

Sinclair sat up and crossed his legs. Kate gently pressed his head down, knowing it would help him gain equilibrium faster.

After a few minutes, he nodded, and they stood up.

"Sinclair, this is Rex. Rex, this is Sinclair," Kate said.

"Hello," Sinclair said. He stared at Rex before asking, "What are you? Where are you from?"

"Do you see a large orange cat?" Kate asked Sinclair. "He changes form. Do you see him as I see him?"

"Good question. I see an avatar cat. But what are you really, Rex?" Sinclair asked.

Rex stared at them with his droll expression. His tail flicked once, but otherwise, he remained still, like a bored cat.

"Why won't he speak, Kate?" Sinclair asked.

"He will. He speaks slowly. He thinks slowly. He moves slowly. It's just the way he is," Kate replied.

After another minute, Rex spoke. "We don't have time for questions. The others are almost here. There will be more violence."

"What others? When?" Kate asked.

"Space Force and NASA have done nothing to clean up the garbage; the dangerous pollution is still there," Rex replied.

"Well, minus the rich dude's car, a few satellites, and a $100,000 toolkit that found their way back to earth. You did get rid of some of it, and you also killed more people," Kate replied, flashing anger. "Sinclair and I are in serious trouble with the government, media, public, and police; your efforts have ruined our lives. No, I don't believe anything has been done about the pollution. When I was being interviewed on Sunday night at Space Force Headquarters, relaying your message as directed, they said they did not have the ability or technology to clean it up and needed time. I think all they've done since then is follow me, hoping I would lead them to you."

Rex took his time before responding, "You are all in danger. They will come and see the situation. They will not accept it. There will be more violence."

"Who is coming? From where?" Sinclair asked.

"What kind of violence, Rex?" Kate asked.

"They might just end it. Violence for everyone responsible for the pollution and collision. Everyone," Rex replied slowly.

"Space Force? NASA? The international and corporate space industry? Like all staff and employees?" Kate asked, trying to make him specify.

"Everyone who benefits from or contributed to the pollution," Rex replied.

"That includes taxpayers and people who use the satellites for TV, for anything from weather reports to national security to communication? Is that what you mean by everyone?" Kate asked, pushing for more clarity.

"Yes," Rex replied slowly.

"Including my mother, Kyle, and Baby Katniss?" Kate asked, still pushing for the scope of the blame.

"Yes, everyone who contributes to and benefits from the pollution," Rex said.

"What exactly happened in the collision?" Sinclair asked.

Rex did not respond.

"Why won't you answer Sinclair? It's a fair question. If we're all going to die, it would be nice to know why. What did the debris, the dangerous pollution, actually do?" Kate asked.

After a few minutes, Rex responded, "Some very important dignitaries, leaders, and heroes in my world were peacefully traveling in this solar system. They were simply observing and learning when their transport was destroyed; they are no more."

"I am very sorry for your loss, Rex, for your world's loss; that is tragic," Kate said.

"It was preventable. They need to clean up the dangerous pollution now. It might appease them. But to do nothing? They will not accept that. Meaningless words don't matter; they will want results," Rex explained.

"Why are you here?" Sinclair asked. "Were you told to communicate with us about the pollution?" He seemed mesmerized by Rex.

"I was the closest to Earth. When I learned of the collision, I came here to see what happened. It took time to understand. Not that there was a collision, that was clear. But why your people would allow it to happen. Was it for primitive security? Was there any meaningful reason?" Rex asked.

All three were quiet.

Rex continued in his slow cadence, "I concluded that there was no reason, just selfish behavior with total disregard for others, even your own kind."

He doesn't seem emotional. He's not in this room. He's somewhere else, and the pace and the lack of emotion are a result of the distance. How did I not realize this before?

"Sounds like humans," Kate said, thinking of other important issues like climate change, the biodiversity extinction crisis, and racial justice. "Well, some humans, but certainly not all. The ones that would think about the impact on the environment, people, animals, nature, and extraterrestrials are never allowed in the room when decisions are made about pollution. The wealthy and powerful make the decisions; the environment, good people, nature, wildlife, and others suffer the consequences. It's not fair. I don't suppose you could tell the others to direct their violence on the deserving? The ones who made all the decisions and make all the money from the deadly pollution? I could make a list," Kate said. "Sinclair can help."

"It won't matter to them. They will not see or understand a difference. Everyone pays for it, everyone uses it, and everyone looks away," Rex said.

"Could you remove the pollution?" Sinclair asked. "We don't have the technology to do it rapidly. It would take months, years even; and that's assuming we could get Space Force and all worldwide space industries to believe and understand the dire situation. It may take even longer to convince them to work together," Sinclair said, sighing and shaking his head. "It would be nearly impossible, but if you have the technology and ability, you could give us like a head start. That would be very helpful."

There was another long pause. No one said anything. Kate was frustrated and exhausted, so she sat down on the white floor.

"I could destroy and remove it, but that will not appease them. They will be disappointed in me; still, your world will suffer," Rex finally replied.

Kate and Sinclair looked at each other; Kate felt a small glimmer of hope.

"Could you effectively remove it in a way that would look like humans were responsible? Is that possible?" Sinclair asked, his voice growing louder with excitement.

Rex was quiet again as they waited with bated breath.

"I should not. Your pollution killed our leaders; they were heroes. They deserve better," Rex finally replied.

"Killing more people will not bring them back. You killed hundreds of millions of people and changed our world forever. You punished the world; every single person on Earth lost someone and has suffered. You avenged your fallen heroes. If you can't convince the others of this, then maybe destroying the pollution and making it look like humans did it will be enough," Kate said, excited by the possibility of preventing more bloodshed.

Suddenly the ground started to shake violently.

"No, Rex, please!" Kate screamed. "We have more questions!"

But it was too late.

THIRTY

Fifty-One Days After the Shooting

Kate and Sinclair landed hard on the couch in Karisma's rental house. Kate landed so forcefully that she bounced off the couch and hit her knees on the coffee table.

"Ouch!" she exclaimed. "Dammit, Rex!"

"Jesus, Kate, look where we are; look what he did! This is amazing! Rex is extraordinary," Sinclair said, looking around in disbelief.

They whipped around to face the front door as they heard keys jingling in the lock.

A young woman walked in. "What the hell!" she exclaimed, startled by the sight of Kate on the floor and Sinclair on the couch.

"I thought you were out since there was no car in the garage!" the woman cried, processing her surprise.

"Is that you, Harriet?" Sinclair asked.

"I know it's been a couple of years, but I haven't changed that much, Uncle Sinclair," she said, putting on a mask covered with hearts. "I would hug you, but I can't."

"You have grown some since I saw you last. Are you still attending the Florida Institute of Technology? Sophomore, right?" Sinclair asked. He was smiling big as he stood up. "Shoot, let me find a mask."

"Yes, I suppose; it's been a strange year. I'm only taking two classes online this semester. I mostly work for my mom. I'll go back full-time when the pandemic is over, or my mom would kill me. She wants me to be like Aunt Yvette, now more than ever. Oh, I am so, so sorry for your loss!" Harriet said. "I haven't really talked to you since before July 14. That zoom thing was not a proper memorial. I honestly can't believe she's gone!" Harriet's eyes started to water.

"It's okay, Harriet. We are living in the most heartbreaking times. Kate and I are here researching some of Yvette's work. It's been distracting and helpful. Much better than being alone in D.C.," Sinclair said.

"Of course. That makes sense," Harriet said, wiping her eyes.

"So, Mom sent me over to give you some of Larry's clothes. I grabbed some shorts, shirts, and new boxer shorts; they were a holiday gag gift. I have no idea if they will fit, but Mom said to try it. She hasn't brought herself to sort through his clothes yet, but she wants you to have them if they fit. I can get jeans and dressy stuff if you want. It's just so damn hot, I thought casual was best," Harriet said, tossing him a bag.

"Thanks, I'll try them," Sinclair said.

"Where is the CR-V?" Harriet asked.

"Oh, right, it's still at Kennedy," Sinclair said.

"I don't think we should get it today. Let's go back tomorrow," Kate said, sitting on the couch and rubbing her knees. Her voice was slightly elevated, still jacked-up from being dropped on the couch only moments before.

It's surreal having this normal conversation after what we just experienced. I have no idea how Sinclair is acting so cool.

Harriet looked at Kate quizzically but didn't ask anything. "I saw one of those doctors who works for the National Institute of Health on TV this morning. He's an expert on the virus. He was saying that Kate and Rex, if they caused the mass shooting, also may have pissed off the virus."

"What does that mean?" Sinclair asked.

"The doctor was saying the virus needs to spread fast; that is how it survives, especially since it kills a lot of its hosts. It needs to jump to its next victim quickly. The masks and social distancing are slowing it down, but it's still infecting people. When Rex and Kate caused the mass shooting, hundreds of millions of people died, and all those vectors and hosts are gone. He said the coronavirus would probably be very angry with them if it felt emotions. Probably be mad at you too, Uncle Sinclair, if it knew you were helping her," Harriet said.

"Wow, I had no idea how powerful I am. I can even piss off a deadly virus," Kate said, smiling at Harriet. She wasn't wearing her mask and had no idea where it was.

"Let me drive you over to Mom's place; she'll make you dinner," Harriet said, staring at Kate.

"That sounds fantastic. Let me freshen up. I'm starving," Kate said, jumping up from the couch and heading to her room. Coming down off the adrenaline left her feeling ravenous. She could tell Sinclair was a little amped up too.

Did we really run for our lives and be saved by Rex only to be told that everyone we love might soon be killed? Did that just happen? Thank the gods Sinclair is with me, or I would be seriously questioning my sanity right now rather than thinking about food.

An hour later, after a stop at a desolate Target, Kate was sitting at a table on the beach, facing the ocean with a cold beer in her hand. She kicked off her shoes and rubbed her feet in the hot sand. She had on clean underwear, bra, t-shirt, and shorts and had more new clothes in a bag at her feet. She watched the distant waves crashing on the land. She was lost in thought about her unbelievable day and what they were going to do next.

"We need to talk about what happened today and create a plan," Sinclair said to Kate.

Yep, he can read my mind. She just nodded in agreement and took a sip of beer.

Karisma came by and took their orders. She was very disappointed that Kate was vegan. She knew Sinclair did not eat meat but was hoping to make fresh fish for Kate. She went into the kitchen to whip up some fancy salads.

"The beach is so empty. This town is so empty. I just can't accept the quiet emptiness. It's making me anxious like a hurricane is coming," Kate said.

"The events of the day might be contributing to your anxiousness," Sinclair said. "What the hell happened today?" he asked, watching the ocean.

Kate smiled at him and said, "We shook our Space Force tail, we found things from outer space in the hangar, our lives were threatened, we ran for our lives, you met Rex, and I think we may have found a solution to prevent more violence. Your idea to have Rex destroy the pollution is a win for everyone. The others won't kill us. It'll make space safer for our astronauts and satellites, Rex, and all traveling dignitaries in space. We have to convince him it's a good plan."

"That depends on what Rex considers pollution," Sinclair said.

"That's true. We do need to talk to him again to convince him that this can work. We have to tell him where and what is pollution, and convince him to destroy all the dangerous debris," Kate said, taking a swig. "And why aren't they here, Sinclair? Space Force, Jack, the cops? They must know we're here because we have our phones. It doesn't make sense. I wonder if they know Rex picked us up and put us down at the rental."

"Maybe they are trying to figure out what happened. If we were running across that huge, empty parking lot toward the woods and just disappeared, they're probably struggling with what happened. You don't know how it looks right? What do people see? I can't believe I met Rex today! I am still trying to process that I met an extraterrestrial, or at least its avatar. Amazing," Sinclair said.

Karisma came out with so much delicious food that Kate applauded. There were salads and bean tacos and homemade salsa. Kate dug in with relish. Karisma also brought more beers. She sat with them, watching them devour the food in silence.

"Okay, now that you're full, where's my car?" Karisma asked.

"At Kennedy. Maybe Anton or Harriet can drive us over there tomorrow to get it?" Sinclair asked.

"How did you get back to the house?" Karisma asked.

"Some strange guy wanted us off the property and returned us to the rental, but we aren't giving up. I work for NASA, Yvette worked for NASA, and I have every right to be there," Sinclair responded.

"Damn right you do!" Karisma said. "I'll have Harriet run you over there in the morning. She's only taking two classes and has time. I can't wait for this nightmare to end. What is left of the people here are pretty worried about COVID. They wear masks and social distance, so hopefully the nightmare passes soon. In Florida, there was a strong correlation between people who died in the shooting and people who refused to wear masks. My Larry fumed about having to wear a mask. He was always ranting about how much money I was losing here, at my other bars, and the rentals because of hysteria about the virus. He was a kind man who loved me and Harriet, but his Florida roots made him listen to that creep in the White House sometimes. He would be shocked by the state of the world now."

Karisma paused to drink some beer before continuing, "We lost our governor, most of the cabinet, and most of our elected officials at every level. But not all of them, and things seem to be working. The world keeps spinning, even though there are way fewer of us."

Kate thought about Rex's threat. *How many innocent lives will be lost if we can't satisfy his, or rather the others', wishes?*

"I sure wish Yvette had gotten rid of that gun. I still can't believe she's gone, especially after being here, with you, Karisma. She should be sitting with us enjoying a beer right now," Sinclair said, staring out at the ocean. "She traveled so often; it's just bad luck that she was home on the 14th."

"She's the reason I live here," Karisma said to Kate. "Yvette and Sinclair had finished school and were living not far from here, working at Kennedy Space Center. My mom thought Yvette was too high and mighty, so I kind of thought she was too. I loved my baby sister and was proud of her, but we weren't particularly close growing up. I was into partying and drugs and lacked focus, the exact opposite of Yvette. Anyway, during one freezing day in Detroit, I said 'fuck it' and drove down to Florida to defrost and see my sister. I loved it here immediately; it was paradise, so I never went back to Michigan. Well, except to get Harriet and for some holidays and family events."

"And you have been so successful owning your restaurants here. This place is fantastic. The rental we are staying at is wonderful. You seem as much the successful businesswoman in hospitality as Yvette was in space exploration," Kate said.

Karisma and Sinclair laughed. Kate did not understand why.

"When I first arrived, Yvette and Sinclair welcomed me with open arms and a free guest room, but I brought my old, self-destructive ways with me. Within months, I was on dope again, using in the warm sunshine rather than in frigid Detroit. I moved out and got my own crappy apartment. I danced for a couple of years at a club near Melbourne. I rarely spoke to Yvette at that time. She was angry with me. I met Larry when I was dancing, and he taught me to manage the bar and restaurant. He helped me get off drugs and went with me to get Harriet in Detroit since I had left her with my mom. Just as we were doing really well, Yvette and Sinclair were transferred to California. Anyway, my baby sister and Sinclair lent me money to open my first bar. They helped me with all this success but only got to enjoy it on short vacations. I always wished you two would move back here," Karisma said, nodding at Sinclair and taking a chug of beer.

A waitress had been hovering nearby as Karisma talked.

"Is there a problem, Liv? A rush?" Karisma asked, laughing at her own joke. "Kidding, we have not had any kind of a rush since July 13. What's up?"

"There is a crowd at the front, some reporters, police, lots of people. They're looking for someone; I think it's these two," Liv responded.

"Tell them they'll have to wait; I'll be out soon," Karisma said.

After the waitress walked back inside, Karisma said, "You two take a stroll on the beach. I'll get Anton or Harriet to pick you up about a mile down. Walk south and watch for my texts. I'll delay them."

"Thanks, Karisma. Dinner was delicious," Kate said.

Kate and Sinclair quickly grabbed their bags and hustled down the beach.

THIRTY-ONE

Fifty-Two Days After the Shooting

Kate slept straight through the night and woke up feeling more rested than she had in weeks; she could not recall a single nightmare. She stretched, rolled over, and was not surprised to find Sinclair gone.

I should not have fallen asleep in bed with Sinclair. I need to work on my boundaries, but I sleep better and feel much safer near him.

Kate freshened up and walked into the kitchen to find Sinclair working on two laptops at once.

"I made coffee, and there's some fruit and bread. How are you feeling?" Sinclair asked without looking up from the computer.

"Good. I slept well, which is kind of crazy considering everything. Well, I think having hope helped me sleep. Hope that we may actually be able to prevent more violence," Kate said, pouring coffee and making toast. "Sorry about crashing with you; I was just so tired."

"No problem, Kate. I slept well too, but we are far from out of danger. Space Force, NASA, police, mobs, and who knows who else may appear at the door at any minute. I have spent the past two hours trying to find a database of all the space junk, or dangerous pollution, that Rex needs to remove. We can't expect him to know the extent of our incompetence and pollution, and we can't expect him to do everything that needs to be done. We need to help him," Sinclair said.

"Of course. What can we do?" Kate said, sitting down at the table.

"I can't find anything resembling a complete database, not in Yvette's files or on any NASA or Space Force websites, internal or public. NASA's Orbital Debris Program Office has a lot, but it can't be all. We need the world's debris, not just American-made. It's almost like they don't want the public to know the extent of the problem. There are tons of cool pictures showing debris as little lights around Earth. It makes it seem harmless, sort of pretty. I've even searched the best space newsletters and websites, but nothing seems complete," Sinclair said.

"Of course, they don't want the public to know they've been treating space like their own personal municipal dump. Just like how there's a serious oil spill every day, multiple leaks on any given day from pipes and oil rigs all over the world, but the public and press only focus on the really big ones with enormous shocking and dangerous damage. It's the daily ones that cause chronic, accumulative impact damage. There is a site that monitors them. The oil spills. It's infuriating and deserves far more attention than it gets," Kate said, dipping toast into her coffee.

Sinclair looked at Kate and asked, "Who monitors the leaks and spills? What government agency collects that information?"

"EPA for inland waters, NOAA for offshore, Interior for land, I think. Most of the big spills and leaks were in the oceans, but they're tracked everywhere now; there are so many leaking pipelines. I think it's NOAA's satellites that track and record all spills. It's so heartbreaking, all those plants, animals, and people being poisoned. We should just put solar panels on every roof," Kate replied.

Sinclair typed away hard for a few minutes. "You're a genius, Kate! It looks like NOAA's satellites also track space debris, and NOAA has a robust database. It's right here. It's public. Well, it looks complete to me. It has more debris details than NASA or makes it more readily available to the public, anyway. It goes back years with lots of information including size, what caused it, and where it might be now. But what if this is just American garbage? I don't know enough about it, and we need to talk to an expert. Hang on," Sinclair said, reaching for Yvette's phone.

Claudia answered and Sinclair put her on speaker. "What's up, Sinclair? Find anything interesting in F-L-A?"

"Yes, Claudia, quite a bit. We found the debris from the collision, at least some of it. You should come down and check it out. It's fascinating, but that's not why I'm calling. Do you know where I can find a complete database of all known space debris? Ours,

China's, Russia, ESA, UAE, private industry, everyone's?" Sinclair asked.

"Huh. Interesting question. You found the materials from the collision and are now trying to find what may have caused it? Can't you tell from what hit what?" Claudia asked.

"It's more complicated than that," Sinclair said.

"Okay. Well, then the Commerce Department, NOAA. They collect all kinds of data, including space debris. I heard the Department of Defense thought it was beneath them because they do important work like defending America. Space Force has no idea what it's doing. NASA has a program office on debris and lots of information. They should have everything you need and make it public, but I don't think they do. Who knows? Maybe NASA wants plausible deniability for when something goes wrong. Anyway, NOAA collects all kinds of data. They collect climate change data, extreme weather, oil spills, and space debris," Claudia replied.

"Interesting," Sinclair said, winking at Kate.

"You know, I have a friend there. He works with the woman that manages the database. If you need more information about that data, she could help. She might enjoy the interest in her work. If I'm recalling correctly, my friend said she gets very frustrated by the lack of concern about how dangerous debris is."

"Great," Sinclair said, "can you get me her contact info?"

"Let me find it, and I'll text it to you," Claudia said.

"Thank you. That will be very, very helpful," Sinclair said.

"Okay, stay safe Sinclair, and say hi to Katie Stellute for me," Claudia said before handing up.

"She hates me," Kate said.

Sinclair sighed. "It doesn't matter now, Kate. If we can get a complete list of debris and get the information to Rex, we might avert a crisis. If we can convince Rex to destroy the debris before his boss arrives, we might dodge a bullet, literally. However, I am a little concerned that the database is enormous, and we don't know what he's capable of."

"He killed hundreds of millions of people all over Earth in fifteen minutes; I think he can clean up our mess in space. At least I hope he can, and will," Kate said, her shoulders tensing again. They were putting a lot of faith in someone, some*thing* they didn't know how to reach.

"While we are waiting on Claudia, let's get ready and head to Kennedy to get Karisma's car. We can talk to Space Force and hope like crazy we see Rex. Is there any way you can communicate with him? We need to convince him that he can and must do this," Sinclair said.

"Are you mad?" Kate asked. "Do you want to go to jail? First of all, we cannot go back to Kennedy, not now. And I don't know how to reach Rex; that's the whole problem."

Sinclair's being ridiculous. Why does he think people who wouldn't reason with us yesterday would suddenly be willing to listen to us today? Just because they witnessed us evaporate into thin air? I don't know if Rex will rescue us again, so I can't put Sinclair in danger.

"If we go to Kennedy, what are we going to do or say that we haven't already said? Tell Space Force and everyone else that has been threatening us that we might have a solution? Ask them for help?" Kate asked.

"For starters," Sinclair said, rubbing his eyes in frustration.

"Come on, Sinclair. Let's say we succeed in convincing Rex to help us with a plan that we don't even know will work. Let's say Rex manages to destroy all the debris, and we save the world from additional violence. Great. We might still be in trouble with the government. They may still need me to take the blame for the shooting; I don't trust them," Kate said.

"But we will prevent more violence and more death, Kate. It's our only hope. We have to work with Space Force and NASA. The choice is to work with them and Rex to stop the violence or die. Why wouldn't we believe Rex? Think about your mom and Kyle. We need to do whatever it takes to save them," Sinclair said.

"Yes, of course. I just hate the idea of working with Space Force; I don't trust them. Space Force and NASA get off easy. They were sloppy and selfish and didn't care what happened to Rex and his people. Their short-sightedness caused enormous problems, not just for other life out there, but for satellites and our astronauts. They knew it, and I'm not surprised Jack and the billionaire space boys don't give a shit. They're just like oil and gas tycoons and every other industry that makes money while regular people suffer the consequences and pay for the clean-up. If it actually ever gets cleaned up. So much does not.

And 70,000,000 Americans paid for that pollution with their lives. Same story, different decade. It's so sad and infuriating. I mean, NASA should have been working with Congress for decades to write laws, real laws with teeth, about preventing the problem and cleaning up the debris, not waiting for a goddammed tragedy to take action!" Kate said, getting angrier as she spoke.

"Yes, you are absolutely right, Kate," Sinclair agreed.

Kate sighed in frustration, pacing the small kitchen. "We also need to tell Rex where all the satellites are, so he doesn't remove the necessary ones. I know of a nonprofit that maintains a database of active satellites in orbit. Last I checked, there were around 2,500 satellites in space, with 2,000 in low Earth orbit. We should share that database with Rex as well."

"I'm sure NASA has that information available. And I do appreciate your lack of trust for government agencies at this point," Sinclair said. "I think Rex knows what's what in space. Three days ago, he made several satellites, one tool kit, and a car crash down on Earth. He didn't need our help finding those," Sinclair reminded her.

"True, but something is still bothering me. Space Force and NASA have knowingly created, basically encouraged, debris in space and ignored it as a problem for decades. Now, you, me, and Rex might clean it up and deal with their mistakes. NASA, the billionaire space boys, and Congress will just move on and act like the whole crisis didn't happen. Space debris is like all pollution, it must be stopped from the source; it can't be more business as usual," Kate said, sighing with frustration.

"True. They have been irrationally irresponsible, and no one has held them accountable. It's infuriating," Sinclair said.

"I don't want NASA or Space Force to be the heroes in this story; they don't deserve it," Kate said, feeling akin to the horrid way she felt when her community made Theo Mast the victim and Kate the bad guy.

They created a false narrative based on lies and convinced the public of their fiction. Corporations do it all the time with help from the politicians they own. They don't care who and what they hurt.

"Let's not get ahead of ourselves; we have to clean up the debris first," Sinclair said.

They both jumped at a loud knock on the front door followed by it slowly opening.

Kate's heart flew into her stomach. "Shit, did we lock the door?" she whispered to Sinclair.

"Good morning," Karisma called as she opened the door and walked into the kitchen. "How did you'll sleep? Oh coffee, thanks," she said, pouring herself a cup.

"Well, thanks. Best sleep I've had in days, despite all the craziness last night," Kate replied with a smile. She really liked Karisma.

"That crowd looking for you was strange: a few reporters, a few cops, and some overly curious regulars. I asked the cops if they had warrants, and they were like, 'No, we just want to ask them a few questions.' I told them, 'Go get a warrant.' We bickered about it being a public restaurant. I told the reporters, 'You can come in, but only when a COVID-safe table opens, and it's a two-drink minimum.' They didn't like that and decided to wait outside. I told them, 'No one likes stalking paparazzi, especially around here.'"

"Don't mess with Karisma," Sinclair said, smiling.

"As for the curious locals and regulars, I asked, 'Why are you hassling my brother-in-law who lost his wife, my baby sister, in the shooting?' I said, 'My brother-in-law is a brilliant scientist, like my deceased sister, and he would not be associated with anyone who caused the mass shooting. He and the woman everyone wants to talk to are trying to figure out what happened!' I told them, 'Stop watching FOX and get off the goddamn internet!'" Karisma was working herself up as she relayed the conversations.

Kate put on a mask as Karisma talked.

"Wow! Thank you! I'm sure Sinclair told you that we had no further problems last night; we found Anton, and he brought us here," Kate said.

"People are so easily manipulated and scared. I only believe what I see with my eyes, in my community, with people I trust. The news, the President, Congress, and Florida lawmakers are all corrupt and looking to make money. They only tell you one side of a story to look good, even if it's not true. When I first saw you on the news as a person of interest, I hoped you were responsible and were caught quickly. I wanted someone to blame and punish. But soon after, I realized it was bullshit; how could a little girl kill hundreds of millions of people? It's not possible," Karisma said.

"What do you think caused it? Any theories?" Kate asked.

"At first, I thought maybe it was biblical. I am a religious woman, and maybe God was judging us. Gun violence is out of control; every day there are mass shootings, gang shootings, and innocents dying. I thought, wow, God nailed it. What better way to get rid of gun violence than to have gun owners kill themselves?" Karisma asked. "But I lost Yvette and Larry, and they were not violent people. They had guns to protect themselves and their families. They needed to protect themselves from the other gun owners, the dangerous, mean, violent gun owners."

Kate winced. The argument that good people with guns need to protect themselves from bad people with guns rang hollow to her. It resulted in far too many guns and far too much death, but she was just listening to Karisma and didn't want to debate.

"But then Sinclair shows up with you, saying Yvette was doing research that might explain the shooting. Once I realized it involved space, it made way more sense than blaming God. Someone screwed something up. I have no idea how, but I sure hope you two will find out," Karisma said. "I also hope whoever caused it gets punished."

Kate smiled.

I do hope NASA and other responsible parties are punished. Rex can't be punished, that's impossible. I just hope we can make sure it never happens again. If we succeed in getting rid of the debris, we need to ensure that Rex doesn't get in trouble with his people, or they might want more revenge. There are millions of pieces of dangerous space debris floating around, and millions of people on Earth who can still be killed.

"Karisma is a great name. I love it; it suits you," Kate said, distracting herself from her dark thoughts.

Karisma sat down at the kitchen table.

"Oh, it was my dancing name. I preferred it to Krystal, my real name. Krystal reminds me of my drug days. My dancing days were way more fun; I learned so much, and it set me on this path to being a successful businesswoman. I met Angelina while dancing; she ran the kitchen. I love Anton like he is my own. And of course, meeting Larry changed my life. We got married, and he adopted Harriet and loved her like his own. So many good things until this horrible year. No one could see this nightmare coming," Karisma said, shaking her head. "I can't believe he's dead."

Sinclair reached for Karisma's hands and squeezed them.

"I'm not obsessed with punishment; I'm New Testament, not Old Testament. I love forgiveness. I just think in this case, we need accountability and punishment to be sure it never happens again. Above all else, we need to try and make sure another mass shooting, or suicide, never, ever happens again."

"I agree. We must prevent more violence," Kate replied. "I was upset before, but talking to you has made me feel better. Thank you, Karisma."

"Of course, Kate, no problem. I'm happy to help, but now I need to go. Sinclair will text Harriet when you all are ready to get my car. I have others, but I love my CR-V," Karisma said as she headed out the door.

Sinclair's phone rang. "It's Claudia."

Kate got a tight feeling in her chest whenever he talked to her.

He put the call on speaker and answered, "Hi, Claudia. That was fast; what did you learn?"

"Bad news. My friend Edmund said that the woman who managed the database left NOAA more than a year ago. While he considered her a friend, he hasn't heard from her since she resigned. He thinks she may have gone to work for the Department of Defense. Sorry, I don't have better news. Edmund is calling around to find her contact information. I remain confident he will find her, just not as quickly as I thought," Claudia said.

"Thanks for trying, Claudia. We appreciate all your help. Let us know when you hear from your friend," Sinclair said, preparing to end the call.

"Hang on! Hi, Claudia, it's Kate. How are you?" Kate interjected.

"Fine, I guess," Claudia responded curtly.

"Do you know Edmund's friend's name?" Kate asked.

"Yes, I wrote it down somewhere," Claudia said. They could hear papers rustling. "Jo-Ellen Marshall."

THIRTY-TWO

Fifty-Two Days After the Shooting

Sinclair looked at Kate and mouthed the words "holy shit" without saying anything out loud, and she looked at Sinclair, eyes wide in surprise.

"Thanks, Claudia. Let us know if Edmund finds her contact information. Stay safe," Sinclair said and quickly hung up.

"It's too much of a coincidence. How many Jo-Ellen's are there? It's an uncommon name. It must be her," Kate said.

"Right. But why? What is her game? This is so peculiar," Sinclair said, pacing as he talked.

"She was so relaxed about our space debris talk on your porch that day. Remember when she was eavesdropping, and she accepted what we were saying without question? To most people, it would have sounded ridiculous or crazy, but she didn't miss a beat. She was more worried about Space Force using me as a scapegoat, or at least that's what she said," Kate said, also pacing around the kitchen. "And the brave comment during the Space Force interview at HQ. What was that about? What's her angle?"

Is Jo-Ellen actually on our side? If so, she has a funny way of showing it. Still, it feels good to think someone on the inside cares about this issue and understands what we need to do.

"Did you ever get her last name?" Sinclair asked.

"No. I'm sure I heard it at some point. Marshall sounds right. I think I heard someone call her Marshall, but I thought it was a job title or joke. I don't like her, so didn't care to know her last name. I feel confident that the NOAA database expert and our Jo-Ellen are one and the same," Kate said. "And to reiterate, I don't think we should go to Kennedy Space Center today. I don't trust those assholes. We need a plan. We need to think this through carefully. We need to talk to Jo-Ellen without anyone around."

"Do you think she'd come alone? Could she come alone?" Sinclair asked.

THIRTY-THREE

Fifty-Two Days After the Shooting

Kate found paper and a pen and wrote down all the details she could recall over the past several days. She wanted to get her head straight and remember everything Jo-Ellen had said. At some point, Sinclair ordered sandwiches, and they both ate in silence, working independently.

Sinclair's phone rang, and they both jumped. It was dark, and Kate turned on the lights as Sinclair spoke to Karisma. This time, he didn't put it on speaker.

"We've been working all day," he said, rubbing his eyes. "No. I promise we'll get it tomorrow. I think it's best if we just stay here." He refilled his water glass. "No, we haven't seen anyone or had anyone knock on the door. It's nice and quiet." He pulled out a bag of chips and opened it, passing it to Kate, whose stomach growled. "No thanks, Karisma; we can order a pizza. We appreciate everything you've done. Okay. Okay. Okay. Thanks. Bye for now," Sinclair said, smiling.

"Karisma is sending over dinner; she is making us something special. A member of her staff, Meg, is bringing it here," Sinclair said.

"Karisma is so nice," Kate said. "What are you working on?"

"Still looking into the collision. Trying to figure out where it happened and what hit what. I'm also finding out what I can about Jo-Ellen Marshall; there's not much online about her," Sinclair responded.

"I have an idea," Kate said.

Kate's phone suddenly rang. "I have to take this," Kate said, answering it and heading into the other room to sit down on the couch.

"Hi, Mom! Where are you? How are you?" Kate asked.

"I'm okay. The kids are okay. I'm staying near their new home and helping everyone get adjusted. The relatives are super nice. They lost a lot of people; the kids lost a lot of people. It's so much heartbreak, but I think everything will be okay eventually. I'm teaching them how to care for Baby Katniss, but that is not why I'm calling, Kate. I listened to your video recording," Kate's mom said quickly.

"And?" Kate asked, standing up and pacing the room.

"Help me understand. You think Rex is an extra-terrestrial avatar that looks like a huge cat, and Rex somehow caused the mass shooting because he was angry about a collision in outer space?" Kate's mom asked.

She knew it sounded unbelievable, but it was the truth. "Yep. That's it in a nutshell," Kate replied.

"Huh. So, someone or something did something really, really bad; they told you they did it, so you told the proper authorities, and you're in trouble? Let me be very clear: you went from a person of interest in a worldwide mass shooting to the cause of it because the proper authorities have decided to blame you for a frickin' worldwide mass shooting? Jesus, Kate, this does remind me of Colorado and that asshole, Theo Mast; I'm not sure if it's Rex or the government in his role this time," Kate's mom said.

"Me neither. We are working on it, but this time I'm taking action and trying to be smarter and proactive. I can't run away again," Kate said. "Sinclair and I have an idea so crazy that it just might work. I do need to go soon; know I'm safe, and we are working hard to find a way out of this mess, ideally without any more violence," Kate told her mom.

"Hang on a sec. First of all, you were a little girl; you did not run away. We removed ourselves from a dangerous situation. Second, I am extremely worried about you. You have an ET and the government after you, and you speak about violence way too casually for me to accept that you're safe," her mom said, her voice getting higher with concern.

Kate laughed and said, "Okay, yes, you're right. It sounds dangerous because it is, but I'll try to be careful. I'll call you tomorrow. I love you."

"I love you too, Kate. I don't understand what is happening, but I have absolute faith you will do the best you can."

As soon as she hung up, Kyle called, but Kate let it go to voicemail; she wasn't in the mood to lie or explain. The call with her mom, who trusted and believed her, made Kate feel at peace and strong and brave. Twenty minutes of explaining the current situation to Kyle, or worse, lying, would ruin her confidence and clarity of purpose.

The only person who truly understands what I'm up against and going through is Sinclair. I have no idea what I would do without him.

THIRTY-FOUR

Fifty-Three Days After
the Shooting

It was just after eight o'clock, and Sinclair and Kate were having a quick breakfast when Anton walked into the kitchen.

He must have a key. I know the door was locked this time.

"Good morning, Anton. Want some coffee? Breakfast?" Kate asked.

"No thanks; I'm good. Am I driving you up to Kennedy?" Anton asked.

"Not now, but we do need another favor. Can you take this on a drive up I-95?" Sinclair said, handing Anton his cell phone.

"Huh? Your phone needs to get out for a while, feeling pent-up?" Anton said with a smile.

"Yes, it's been cooped up for too long," Sinclair said, playing along.

"But seriously, you will be tailed with this phone, most likely by several black SUVs. They will follow for a while, but at some point, they will pull you over," Sinclair said.

Anton's eyebrows shot up in surprise.

"The black SUVs will have several Space Force agents in plain clothes; they have been tailing us since D.C. When they pull you over, tell them Sinclair asked you to take his cell phone for a ride. They will understand. Tell them you have no idea where I am, which is the truth because you won't. They'll be frustrated but not dangerous. If for any reason it gets weird, just say, 'Call Kate; she is expecting your call.' However, it could be the police that are sent after you, and that's a whole different situation."

Anton didn't say a word, but his eyes went from wide in surprise to half-closed and suspicious.

"We came up with a plan which we think will alleviate any problems with the cops. Larry's sister will go with you; she should be here soon," Sinclair said.

Anton shook his head with a slight smile and said, "Okay, that sounds good."

"I was worried about this plan, Anton. I was afraid of the police pulling you over, but Sinclair assured me you'll be safe. Karisma suggested Larry's sister and explained she is a County Commissioner who knows many of the police, at least what is left of them, and that made me feel better. But do you feel safe? You can say no and not do this," Kate said. She truly hated the idea of putting him in a potentially dangerous situation.

Anton smiled and nodded and said, "It's okay, Kate. I feel fine with it."

"We'll pay you for your time, of course," Sinclair added.

"It's all cool," Anton said, still smiling.

There was a knock on the door, and Sinclair went to answer it.

"Is this phone in trouble?" Anton asked Kate, making her laugh.

A very tan and very blonde White woman walked into the kitchen; Kate guessed she was around fifty. She was wearing a mask that read *Made In Brevard*. "Hi, Anton. How are you, honey?" she said, giving him an elbow bump. "I guess we're going on some adventure. Whatever Karisma wants, Karisma gets! Right? Right?" she asked, laughing loudly at her own words.

Anton just shook his head in agreement.

"I'm Nancy, Larry's sister," the woman said to Kate.

"Hi, I'm Kate. Thanks for helping us this morning," Kate replied.

"Sure. No problem," Nancy replied. "You ready, Anton?"

Sinclair walked out to the garage with them. After they drove off in Anton's van, Sinclair returned to the kitchen.

"We better go now," Kate said. "They could get pulled over before they get to 95."

Kate and Sinclair talked as they walked a couple of miles to the bridge that went over the lagoon and led to the beach.

"Nancy seems nice," Kate said.

"She's a character. Born and raised in this county. Karisma and Larry got her elected, and she loves being a commissioner. That's why she said, 'Karisma gets what Karisma wants,'" Sinclair said, mimicking Nancy's drawl.

"I'm happy we left early; it's getting hot already," Kate said as they reached the bridge. In normal times, there would be constant traffic over the causeway, but there were very few cars. As they walked, they often had the whole bridge to themselves and could hear the water splashing on the shore below.

"It's so beautiful," Kate said, watching the sun glisten on the lagoon. "Dolphins! Look!"

"Wow," Sinclair said.

"I miss Florida. When I see all this natural beauty, I miss it so much. It is paradise," Kate said, watching the dolphins swim around. "They must be feeding."

"I wouldn't want to live in a world without dolphins," Sinclair said.

"Me neither," Kate said, taking his hand and squeezing it.

I feel so safe holding Sinclair's hand. I love how we reach for each other; sometimes, it makes me tingle. It must be the constant stress and excitement.

As they walked along, Kate kept talking. "I wonder if the lagoon is cleaner with fewer people? I realize it has only been a couple of months since the shooting. It hasn't been enough time to impact pesticides, fertilizers, and cattle manure runoff, but Florida lost more than seven million people on July 14. Seven million people create a lot of waste from septic tanks that leak into springs, rivers, canals, and lagoons. It would be nice if something good, like less pollution, came from the tragedy. Cut nature a break," Kate said.

"Yes, I agree. It would be nice if something good came from it. It goes beyond septic tank waste; think about seven million people not producing garbage, cutting down trees and forests, producing global warming gases, or driving their boats into manatees," Sinclair added.

We're always on the same wavelength. I've never felt so close to someone in my life.

"Sinclair, I don't mean to sound harsh or heartless. I wish like crazy it never happened; I wish Yvette and Larry and so many others were still alive," Kate said, fearing that she may have hurt Sinclair with her comments, seeming callous about the loss.

"I know, Kate. If something good comes out of this nightmare, I'm all for it. If it helps nature and wildlife, it helps people; we are all connected. Maybe we will regain balance," Sinclair said, still holding her hand.

Their conversation was interrupted when an SUV pulled over in front of them, blocking the bike path they were walking on.

"What the hell?" Jo-Ellen said, rolling down the window. "Get in. Now!"

"Are you alone?" Kate asked.

"Yes. Please get in!" Jo-Ellen said, sounding upset.

"Our plan is working," Kate whispered to Sinclair as they got in the SUV.

THIRTY-FIVE

Fifty-Three Days After the Shooting

"**W**hat are you doing?" Jo-Ellen asked, but she didn't wait for an answer. "As soon as I realized you were going in separate directions, I sent the team after Sinclair, and I came for you, Kate. I figured Kate was running, so imagine my surprise finding both of you taking a morning stroll over the causeway. You know we are watching you, and you know why." She was interrupted by her phone ringing.

"Hello. What's up?" Jo-Ellen asked. "You found his phone but no Sinclair?"

Kate shook her head vigorously, and put her finger to her lips, silently pleading with Jo-Ellen not to say another word.

Jo-Ellen paused, listening to someone on the phone.

"Well, I have eyes on Kate, Tonya. I suggest you double back and find Sinclair. Call me when you have him," Jo-Ellen said and ended the call.

"Let's go to the beach and take a walk," Kate said to Jo-Ellen. "We aren't saying another word until we get to the beach."

Twenty minutes later, the three were walking slowly down the beach, carrying their shoes and watching the waves break. Kate insisted that all phones were left in the car.

"It's so breezy near the water, I doubt we need these," Kate said, taking off her mask.

"Enough already. What's going on?" Jo-Ellen demanded.

"You are Jo-Ellen Marshall, former NOAA employee who cataloged space debris," Sinclair stated.

Jo-Ellen's eyebrows rose, making her seem surprised, but the small smirk on her lips indicated she was not.

"Yep. I did it for a few years, but they shifted the database to the Department of Defense. I moved to Space Force, hoping I would get assigned to it again, but the DOD didn't want it and moved it to NASA. I planned to transfer to NASA, but July 14 put a pause on the plan," Jo-Ellen replied.

"Why do you like tracking space debris?" Sinclair asked.

"Because it is an enormous problem which puts all astronauts, all satellites, and all equipment at risk. Space tourists are supposed to be going to the Space Station starting next year. It's a big deal, but no one in power cares. I worry they'll bury the database and the information," Jo-Ellen said with more passion in her voice than Kate had ever heard.

"Have you seen the debris in the hanger at Kennedy?" Sinclair asked.

"Yes, I've been in there, but I don't know if it's been entered correctly in the database; it's always an afterthought. If no one insists it gets filed correctly, it might not get done. Especially because that debris is, how should I say it, *special*," Jo-Ellen said. "I've seen it in relation to luring you all into the hangar as a Space Force Agent, not an analyst. They wanted to see what you would do."

"What we would do, or what Rex would do?" Kate asked.

"Rex. They've been following you to get to him. Ever since you got in the car at Space Force HQ with Sinclair, we've been following you," Jo-Ellen said. "They were so pissed when they lost you in the woods. I was so pissed, searching through the wetlands covered in mosquitos; I'm terrified of snakes and alligators. I told you, I am an inside person."

"Lost us? Running across that huge parking lot? We made it to the woods?" Kate asked. "You have to know that doesn't make sense. We don't run that fast."

Jo-Ellen stopped walking. "When we got to the back of the building, you were out of sight."

"We didn't make it to the woods, Jo-Ellen," Kate said.

"Rex?" she asked.

Kate nodded.

"I knew you couldn't make it to the woods that fast. Others were convinced that it was feasible since you're athletes, runners, but I didn't buy that bullshit. But what could I do? I work for them," Jo-Ellen said.

"They overestimated our athletic prowess," Sinclair said.

"Hey, I do run fast," Kate said, slapping his strong biceps with the back of her hand.

"None of it made sense, but everyone in that parking lot was very stressed, so I just did as I was told," Jo-Ellen said. "So, what really happened?"

"Rex grabbed us, and we were in the white room. He was more upset than ever before and warned us that we are all in danger. He said *they* will come and see the situation and there will be more violence," Kate said.

"Who?" Jo-Ellen asked.

"His big space bosses, of course," Sinclair said.

"Rex didn't give us names. He said, '*They* might just end it.' *End it*," Kate emphasized, getting goose-bumps repeating the terrible message.

"What did Rex mean by that?" Jo-Ellen asked.

"Rex said, 'Violence on everyone responsible for the pollution. Everyone. Everyone who benefits from or contributed to the pollution.' Which is everyone on the planet," Kate elaborated.

Sinclair added, "I asked Rex exactly what happened in the collision, and he explained that some very important dignitaries from his planet, heroes, were peacefully traveling, observing, and learning, and their transport was destroyed. They died."

"That's terrible," Jo-Ellen said. "Fucking debris. I knew something terrible would happen. I didn't think it would happen to extraterrestrials though, but I guess it makes sense."

"Rex said, 'Their deaths were preventable if we would have cleaned up our pollution.' He was angry about the debris, especially since it stems from lazy, selfish behavior. He's right. He explained to us that the others might be appeased if we clean it up fast," Sinclair said.

"Of course, he is right. Everyone at NASA knows that the debris is a timebomb waiting to explode; we're playing Russian roulette up there. Damn, and now 70,000,000 Americans have paid the price. What can be more violent than that?" Jo-Ellen said, shaking her head.

"I asked Rex if he could remove the pollution," Sinclair said. "I told him we don't have the technology to do it, much less the ability to do it quickly. It would take months, years, assuming we could get Space Force and all worldwide space agencies and industries to focus, and then we'd have to convince them to work together. It's nearly impossible. But if Rex has the technology now, he could give us a head start."

Hearing Sinclair share the plan solidifies that it's the right move, really the only move. If only I could summon Rex at will. All those times I was afraid to see him, and now, I wish he would come and take all three of us to the white room.

"That's a great idea. What did he say?" Jo-Ellen asked.

"He didn't seem convinced," Kate said, "but we want to ask him again; we have to persuade him it's the right thing to do."

Kate and Sinclair stared at Jo-Ellen.

Okay, Jo-Ellen, this is your part. If you're an expert on the amount and location of the debris, I hope you know the most about how to get rid of it. We need you to know what to do next.

Jo-Ellen didn't say anything for a few minutes. They stopped walking when they were speaking to each other, but Jo-Ellen had started walking slowly down the beach. Sinclair and Kate dropped back a few steps and followed her.

Kate felt her stomach flutter watching Jo-Ellen.

It's shocking news. We had a whole day to process it, and we just dropped it on her. I hope she will help us. We need to give her time to think, hell, to decide if she even believes us.

After a while, Jo-Ellen turned around to Kate and Sinclair and said, "Maybe he could remove it, destroy it, and do so in a way that looks like humans did it. Not necessarily from Earth and not necessarily using our technology."

Both Kate and Sinclair nodded yes enthusiastically.

"Is that possible?" Sinclair asked, his voice loud with excitement.

"Rex killed 70,000,000 Americans, and you're asking if it's possible to trick whatever is coming to punish the rest of us into not killing us? I'm not sure, but I sure as hell know we need to try. Let's go back to the car; I need to make some calls," Jo-Ellen said, jogging slowly toward the parking lot.

THIRTY-SIX

Fifty-Three Days After
the Shooting

Jo-Ellen was on the phone, walking around the beach parking lot. It was on speaker, so Sinclair and Kate could hear as they followed along beside her.

"Hi, Otter, it's Jo-Ellen Marshall. How are you?" Jo-Ellen asked.

"Jo-Ellen, it's been a long time. What, a couple of years now? I'm fine. How are you? Staying alive, I guess," a man with a strong Scottish brogue said into the phone.

"Fine, fine. I managed to survive the mass shooting and have not gotten COVID, so I guess better than fine," Jo-Ellen replied. "Otter, I need to cut to the chase. I don't know if you know, but I left Commerce a while ago and moved to Space Force. You might say that I was literally chasing debris. Anyway, I still follow your work, of course. I know you won't reveal your real progress, or lack of, in public. Can you tell me, what exactly is the current status of destroying space debris and garbage?" Jo-Ellen asked.

"First, my dear, the space industry does not like the word garbage. It makes it sound like they are litter-bugs and not respecting space," Otter replied.

"They are and they don't, as you well know," Jo-Ellen replied.

Otter laughed. "In short, similar place as always, but making progress. We need a strong, precise laser able to pulverize debris ranging in size from a soft-ball to .000039 of an inch in diameter. As you know, there are more than 100 million pieces of potentially dangerous manmade debris in space. We don't have a strong enough laser yet. We have 3-D smart glasses which are grand, but still too weak, even with the best optical telescopes. We are making progress with new tech breakthroughs all the time, but I would esti-mate that we are a year or two away from real-world clean-up," Otter replied.

Kate's shoulders slumped. *That's not promising.*

"Now I remember why I get frustrated with your industry; it's always a year or two away from a real prototype, much less commercialization. I know you're the best of the best, but I need to ask: Do any other companies have more advanced tech? Any competi-tors you are monitoring because you honestly think they are pulling ahead? What about the billionaire space boys? What are they doing?" Jo-Ellen asked.

"No. No competitor that I know of is anywhere near us. As for the billionaires, they are obsessed with being showcased in the media and beating each other into space to recoup their money through tourism.

They have zero interest in clean-up, but I bet they will when I have a viable prototype, and they realize there is profit in it. They will try to swoop in and swallow our industry whole; they are such entitled pricks," Otter said.

Jo-Ellen sighed loudly and said, "It's always about the money. Everything is about the money."

"What's going on? Why the sudden interest in my work? I know you are passionate about debris, but you sound angrier and more anxious than I remember. Has there been another collision?" Otter asked.

"We are in a crisis to get some debris cleaned up now. I am going to call you tomorrow when I get my hands on some pretty advanced tech. I'll need you to tell me how to put it together and make it work; I'll need to know what location to place the laser. This is urgent; people's lives are in danger," Jo-Ellen said.

"Jesus Christ. I want to help Jo, but there is no way we can do it, much less do it quickly," Otter said.

"Send me the specs on what you are working on now. I need all your prototype information, so I know what to get for you. I will text where to send it in a minute. I'll meet you virtually tomorrow on a secure line and show you what we have, so we can discuss how to make this work. Make yourself available; be at your lab. Astronauts' lives are in danger," Jo-Ellen said and hung up.

Sinclair and Kate stared at her.

"What? I need him to work with urgency," Jo-Ellen said with a shrug.

"What's next?" Kate asked

"Hey, one thing that sticks in my craw--okay, there are many things I'm wondering about--this is all mind-blowing, but why, if Rex is so advanced to get millions of people to shoot themselves, and he can move through space with ease, why is debris so dangerous to his kind? You would think such a creature could easily avoid or manipulate it? Especially if we think he can destroy it now," Jo-Ellen said, not answering Kate's question.

"I've wondered about that myself. Don't know. Hopefully, we can talk to Rex and ask him. But for now, we need to move forward and act on what we know," Sinclair replied.

"Yes, right. Tomorrow, we will go to Kennedy and see if what Otter needs is in that hangar," Jo-Ellen said. "Then, we need to assemble something that looks like it could work. We need Rex's friends to think, or I guess believe, we're getting rid of the debris."

Sinclair nodded.

"Let's go. I need my computers. We can work at your rental," Jo-Ellen said, heading to the car.

"How will we keep Space Force and others away while we work?" Sinclair asked.

"Let me handle them; I'll call Tonya," Jo-Ellen said. "We need to get my computers from my rental, but we can't work there. It has to be your place. Otherwise, Space Force could barge in and try to take over and do stupid things. Again."

Kate smiled at Jo-Ellen.

I never expected to have a comrade in Jo-Ellen. I love that our team is growing.

THIRTY-SEVEN

Fifty-Three Days After the Shooting

Jo-Ellen told Tonya and Space Force she was personally guarding Kate and Sinclair because of the morning's antics. Kate wanted to trust Jo-Ellen, and so far, her actions indicated she was on their team.

"Jo-Ellen, when I was being interviewed, more like interrogated, at Space Force, you said I was 'brave.' Why did you say that?" Kate asked.

"Right before the interview, someone handed me a copy of a list you had written at some point. Space Force thought it was evidence you were communicating with Rex, which it was. Since I had spoken to you on Sinclair's back porch, I knew everything on the list. Well, except for that brave comment. I did not understand that. I just said it to you to get a reaction. In the interview, you told everyone at Space Force what was on the list with more details. Guess that is why your list was not discussed again, at least not with me," Jo-Ellen said, as she opened her computer.

"So, you hacked into my personal computer?" Kate asked, annoyed but not surprised.

Jo-Ellen looked up at Kate and said, "No, not me, but someone at Space Force. I told you they were tracking you because they're obsessed with Rex. I am sorry about it now; it was a total violation of privacy and trust. You didn't deserve it since you were completely truthful at the interview."

"Okay, guess I figured that was the case. And it doesn't matter now anyway," Kate said.

But it did matter to Kate. It further proved she could trust Jo-Ellen.

Late into the evening, Sinclair and Jo-Ellen stared at their computer screens, studying the information Otter sent and the collision material reports Sinclair had. They also referenced Jo-Ellen's debris database.

"It's not up-to-date; I don't have any new data in almost two years. That's a problem," Jo-Ellen said to Sinclair.

"Even if we only remove the debris you logged in before you left NOAA, it would be huge. Let's worry about the complete database later," Sinclair said.

Realizing she couldn't help in any way, Kate went to her bedroom to check in with her mom. Kate was relieved to hear her mother was staying in Tennessee for a few more days. She missed her and wanted her in Florida, but knew it was best to stay away until the crisis was resolved. Kate didn't want anyone, not Space Force, police, or the media, using her mother to get to her. Her mom spoke mostly about the kids and didn't ask any questions about Rex or Space Force.

There are probably other people around and she doesn't want them to hear her asking me certain questions.

After she hung up with her mom, Kate sighed deeply and called Kyle.

"Kate! How are you? I've been worried," Kyle said as soon as he answered.

"I'm good. I'm safe. How are you, babe?" Kate asked.

"Okay, I guess. I miss you. It's been a week. Where are you? What are you doing?" Kyle asked.

"Have there been any more mobs at the house? Bricks in the windows?" Kate asked, attempting to delay responding to his questions.

"No, every day since last Monday there have been fewer and fewer people. No one as of yesterday, not even a TV van. The reduction seems to correlate with your coverage on TV. You haven't been on CNN or mainstream media in a few days, but you're still all over FOX and the internet. Amanda and I have been tracking it. By tomorrow, there might not even be a reason for her to check in," Kyle said. "Amanda has been awesome; we have had great talks. You know how you and I always wondered why the police are not supportive of strict gun regulations? Why would cops want spouse abusers and mentally unstable and emotionally immature people to be armed? Why do they support extreme NRA stuff like casual gun sales at flea markets and between friends and family? Well, I got to ask Amanda and her answers were interesting,"

"What did she say?" Kate asked.

"Well, Amanda is a very young, new cop, and she was working a desk job before the shooting; she didn't have her own personal gun, so she did not shoot herself on July 14. I will also add that she is Black, and her grandfather and uncle were D.C. cops too, so she has a good perspective; she has inherited experience, even though she is so young. Anyway, she said she supports an assault weapons ban. She thinks it's outrageous that civilians have assault weapons. She supports background checks, extensive rules, training, and protocols before an American can own a gun, with the hope that the hurdles will weed out irresponsible gun owners. She also thinks we need far more mental healthcare, especially in low-income and poor communities because of systemic neglect," Kyle said.

Kate squelched a twinge of jealousy. It sounded like Kyle and Amanda were growing close.

Like me and Sinclair.

"That sounds very cool. I wish more cops were like her," Kate said. "Maybe they will be now."

"She said some people who work for the unions are all pro-gun. For example, they think that women with abusers in the house should have a gun to protect themselves. They say everyone with a gun just has it to protect themselves. Living in total fantasy land, like the abuser won't take her gun and shoot her. Or like gun owners in cities won't end up victims of crimes like robbery and lose their guns to gangbanger assholes who shoot bystanders by accident. Right? Anyway, Amanda says some in the union repeat NRA talking points and stereotypes and bullshit. She says toxic cops love it and don't question it. And if good cops do, they are made to understand that the union will not necessarily be there for them. It's implied that if they are in a car accident, hurt their back, or get shot, some in the union might not fight too hard for them. She says it can be sinister," Kyle said.

"Damn, and she works in a more liberal, pre-dominantly Black police force. I bet it's really easy for union reps to intimidate good cops in Alabama, Florida, Louisiana, and many other gun-loving states," Kate replied.

"Amanda just hopes the shooting changes gun ownership in America. We have great conversations; I love the insight into the mind of an honest cop," Kyle said.

Kate pulled her brows together and cocked her head. *Is Kyle too enthusiastic about Amanda's insights?*

"Anyway, did you find your harasser?" Kyle said, changing the subject.

"We are still working on it. We're in Florida now and pretty close to a breakthrough," Kate said.

"Look, Kate, I'm trying to be supportive, but I think you and Sinclair chasing leads to find an unstable space junkie is at best a long-shot, at worst, a big waste of time. I thought it seemed a little pointless at the beginning, but I figured it was better for you to do something; you like to take action, I get it. But now, I think it's just a long, distracting road trip and maybe it's time to come home. Maybe Space Force and the other government authorities are pursuing another lead. A better lead.," Kyle said.

"If I don't solve this, they will blame it on me," Kate said. "The country needs someone to place their heartbreak, blame, and hate on. Also, it's important to me. I'm doing something good, Kyle."

"What's important?" Kyle asked. "How will you solve this? I don't understand."

I feel terrible. Should I send him the video that I sent my mom? I could just pour out the whole story. So much has happened, and I'm tired just thinking about it. I don't have the energy to explain why I've been lying to him.

"Amanda says your story is full of holes; she says it doesn't make any sense, and you aren't telling me everything," Kyle said.

"What? Kyle, you told Amanda? I asked you to not tell anyone. Why would you do that?" Kate asked, shocked that he'd defy her trust with someone he just met.

This is why I did not tell you the truth in the first place. My instincts were right!

"She's a cop. I figured she would have some good advice, and she did," Kyle responded defensively.

"Okay babe, I need to go. I hope to be home in a few days. When this is over, we can talk, and everything will be okay. Okay?" Kate said, trying to be optimistic. She felt deflated just thinking of returning home and explaining everything to Kyle. She knew he would be skeptical and need to be convinced of so much.

"Exactly when will you be home?" Kyle asked.

"As soon as I can," Kate said.

Well, assuming we manage to save the world from Rex's cohorts.

THIRTY-EIGHT

Fifty-Four Days After the Shooting

The next morning Kate got up early. Sinclair was already up and half a pot of coffee into the day.

"Did you make any progress?" Kate asked.

"Hell yes. We worked all night, and I think we see a way forward. We created a plan. It's the best we can do," Sinclair said, pacing around the kitchen. "There are so many variables we have no control over, but we have to move forward."

Kate surprised Sinclair with a hug. With tears in her eyes, she said, "Thank you, Sinclair. I don't know what I would do without you."

Sinclair hugged her back hard without saying a word.

They both jumped when the back door opened and Karisma walked in.

"Sorry to interrupt, but where's my CR-V?" Karisma asked, laughing. "By the way, I heard Anton and Nancy had an adventure yesterday; they were pulled over on 95 by six black SUVs. I thought you all went to Kennedy? Wait, what did you eat for dinner?"

Sinclair laughed as he explained. "We asked Nancy to go to protect Anton from the police, but it was just Space Force chasing my phone. I heard they were fine; they handed over my phone as we asked them to do. We had some unexpected issues arise yesterday and didn't make it to Kennedy, but we will get your car today. And we ordered pizza."

"Alright, smartass, as long as everyone is safe and sound and my CR-V will be home soon, we are good. Where did you get vegan pizza?" Karisma asked.

Before Sinclair could answer, the door opened again. Jo-Ellen walked in, looked around, and said, "Let's go; we need to get to Kennedy, now."

THIRTY-NINE

Fifty-Four Days After
the Shooting

An hour later, Jo-Ellen, Sinclair, and Kate were
driving to Kennedy Space Center.

"I feel like we should duck or hide or something,"
Kate said from the back seat.

"They know we're coming, Kate. I told Tonya and
the team we need to look at the debris again. I'm sure
there will be many Space Force agents watching us at
the hangar. There's no reason to hide; we have been
watching you all along," Jo-Ellen said, looking at Kate
through the rearview mirror. "They're obsessed with
you leading them to Rex; that's all they care about."

Jo-Ellen flashed her ID at the guard and continued
talking to Kate. "We're cleared to the hangar. Lots of
eyes on us. Cameras everywhere. We are safe until
they get Rex. Everyone is working together."

As they drove to the hangar, they saw dozens of
cars, mostly black SUVs, police cars, security vehicles,
and one flashy, sports car.

"I hope they don't try the redneck cop threat again," Sinclair said.

"Focus on the plan; ignore everything else. We go in, take what we need, and leave," Jo-Ellen said.

"Wait, where are we going? What are we taking?" Kate asked, annoyed she had not received any details beyond getting in the hangar.

"Shush," Jo-Ellen said as she got out of the car.

She didn't speak to anyone as she quickly walked to the front door of the hangar. Kate and Sinclair followed. Once inside, Jo-Ellen and Sinclair moved amongst the information cards and debris, taking pictures.

"Kate, there should be a cart somewhere; get it. We need to take some pieces with us," Jo-Ellen said.

"What? Where?" Kate asked, rushing around the huge room looking for a cart.

No one responded.

Ten minutes later, Kate yelled loudly, "I found something we can use!"

She pushed it over to Sinclair who had collected several objects in a small pile.

"Put everything in the cart that you can carry; some are heavy," Sinclair said, pointing to the pieces in his stack. "I need to find a few more."

"Load it and get over here," Jo-Ellen yelled from another part of the hangar.

Once everything was loaded, Jo-Ellen and Sinclair carefully reviewed the pieces.

"It looks like everything," Sinclair said. "I hope it's everything."

It looked like a bunch of junk to Kate. She couldn't tell one piece from the next except some were big and some were small.

I hope they know what they're doing.

"We're walking out the back door," Jo-Ellen said, indicating Kate and Sinclair should follow her with the cart. Even on wheels, it was heavy and slow-going.

"I'm sure they have people in the back this time, Jo-Ellen," Kate said as she pushed. "The front door is closer, both to us and your vehicle, and this is heavy."

Jo-Ellen didn't respond, though she did hold the door open for them.

They emerged into the hot, blinding sun. It was close to two o'clock and the sun was beating down. Kate winced after being in the dark, cool hangar. "Where to?" she asked.

Just then, several young men ran up to help pull the cart to some very shiny, fancy trucks. Kate tried to pull it away from them and shouted, "What the hell?"

"Jack sent us to help," one man said.

"It's fine, Kate. Jack is allowing us to use his secure laboratory on campus to work on our project. Get in one of the trucks; let's not separate ourselves from these materials," Jo-Ellen said.

Kate didn't trust Jack. After all, he was one of the self-centered billionaire space boys. Sinclair did not seem to trust him either; he hadn't been forth-coming with Jack when they changed their route from Houston to Florida. Besides, Jack stood with the threatening crowd that tried to arrest Sinclair the last time they were here.

Jack is an asshole.

Sinclair's quick nod gave her reassurance to accept the situation.

The men quickly loaded the materials into two trucks. Jo-Ellen jogged over to Tonya and retrieved Sinclair's phone without saying a word and quickly returned to the trucks. Kate and Sinclair jumped into the back of one truck, Jo-Ellen the other.

Kate watched as they drove past the hoard of SUVs and Space Force agents, staff, and leadership. She looked at their faces. Their expressions ranged from incredulousness to anger. The cops looked bored.

"What are we doing?" Kate asked Sinclair.

"We are going to Jack's lab as Jo-Ellen said," Sinclair replied.

"But why is he helping us?" Kate asked.

"It doesn't matter. The only thing that matters is we find a way to get Rex out of this mess. Jo-Ellen told Space Force and Jack that we were going through some motions and activities that could trigger Rex to appear. They want Rex; they are obsessed with him. They aren't paying attention to what we're actually doing," Sinclair said.

A few minutes later, they were at a building on the other side of the space center. The men unloaded the materials from the trucks, put them back on the cart, and pushed it toward the building. Kate, Sinclair, and Jo-Ellen followed closely.

"Welcome, welcome. You will soon enter the most secure lab in the most secure building in America," Jack said, waving them in. "Rex is welcome as well."

As they walked in, Jack greeted them individually in his surfer boy accent. "Hello, Kate Stellute, the Rex whisperer. And Sinclair, husband of my dear friend Yvette, and Jo-Ellen, collector of debris data." He laughed loudly at his comments.

I don't trust this asshole one bit.

"I think he's drunk," Kate whispered to Sinclair.

FORTY

Fifty-Four Days After the Shooting

As soon as the equipment was in the lab, Jo-Ellen asked everyone to leave. Jack threw a fit. There was a lot of back and forth between them which Kate ignored. She was focused on the items, studying each object closely and trying to figure out why they were chosen.

Once the room was empty, Jo-Ellen connected Otter on the screen.

"Hi, Otter, this is Dr. Sinclair Jones, NASA biophysicist and expert on all things from space, and Kate Stellute, Space Force analyst and liaison to Rex," Jo-Ellen said, waving her arms to go along with the introductions. "Kate and Sinclair, meet Dr. Duncan Talisker of Glasgow, Scotland, known affectionately as Otter."

Everyone nodded at each other, and then there was an awkward moment of silence.

"Well," said Otter, "I don't understand exactly what's happening, but if you need to destroy some space debris fast, let me jump in with the problems and reality of the situation. According to NASA's Orbital Debris Program Office, there are around 23,000 pieces of space debris larger than ten centimeters orbiting Earth, including about 3,000 defunct satellites. If any of these bits of space junk slam into each other, the collisions could lead to larger pieces of debris. This could happen at any moment, meaning more debris, or garbage, could be created as we speak. Our goal at my company is to turn space garbage into harmless clouds of particles called plasma. We are creating a process of removing materials from a solid surface by irradiating it with a laser beam, obliterating dead satellites and other debris. Some people think we can simply point lasers from the ground into space to zap useless satellites and debris, but all satellite parts are different and carry various risks. For example, the solar cells that satellites use for power could potentially be dangerous. If a laser pings the surface of a solar array, it could eject thousands of shards of glass, creating a cloud of microscopic debris. We would need a space-borne laser to get around these risks. We have been experimenting with different spacecraft materials to see how each reacts to laser pulse emissions irradiation. We need precise lasers, but lasers originating from Earth are subject to atmospheric interference that can decrease the beam's point accuracy. If we had space-based lasers, they could more precisely target satellites while avoiding solar arrays. They would also require less energy."

Otter paused, waiting for a comment or question. When no one spoke, he continued. "Bloody hell, it's not possible. We don't have the range of knowledge to know what laser needs to hit what materials at what exact moment in time. This shit is moving! And the laser can't be on Earth; it must be in space. Too many variables we can't control down here, and our lasers aren't powerful enough," Otter said. "I'm sorry for the bad news, but this is the reality."

"We have new materials and technology right here in this room that can resolve the precision issue. With my knowledge of the location, movement, and speed of the debris, we can locate and hit most of it of all sizes. This tech will help us create a more powerful laser and scope. We will turn all the debris into plasma. All we need to do is put it together," Jo-Ellen said.

Wow, Jo-Ellen is amazing! She seems so confident, almost arrogant, especially considering we have no idea if this will work.

After some more debating about the situation, Kate tuned them out. She didn't understand what they were saying; she wasn't an engineer. When they went off to use the 3-D printer to create Otter's existing prototype, she went into a corner of the lab and found a couch. She sat down to check her email and texts. She decided to email her mom, Kyle, and other friends and family the reasons she loved them, just in case this did not work.

Of course, if this doesn't work, we're all toast.

A couple of hours passed, and Kate found a Space Force agent and asked him to get them food. She was happy to be helpful in some way.

"How will we get it into space? I agree with Otter; there's no way we can plausibly do this from here," Sinclair said to Jo-Ellen when Kate approached them.

Kate detected frustration in his usually patient and calm voice.

"Fuck. What is launching today? If Jack had something going up, we would know," Jo-Ellen said, sounding exasperated. "There's a launch every other day, hence all the garbage and debris, but the day we need one, nothing?"

"Apologies my American friends, but I still don't think this will work. Where did you get these materials? What is going on?" Otter asked from the large screen.

"We learned a lot in that massive collision last year, but we didn't understand it until very recently. Trust us, Otter, it's all good," Jo-Ellen said.

"Like UFO extraterrestrial tech? This stuff is from the collision? What hit what?" Otter asked, his voice rising with excitement.

No one replied.

Why did it take him this long to figure out this is extraterrestrial tech? He must be in denial because he seems really smart.

"What about the Boston billionaire space boy? He launches all the time. Maybe he can push something up. Take a cargo load to the space station today?" Kate asked.

Sinclair reached for his phone and dialed. A second later, Jack was on a screen, frantically looking around the room.

"What is going on? You're in my lab, and I demand to know, dude! Sinclair, you better be working for me, on my side, or…"

"Jack, sorry to interrupt, but we need your help again," Sinclair said, cutting off Jack's rant.

Jack went quiet but looked angry.

"We need to get a load to the space station today. Who's going up? It's an emergency. No one but you and your staff will see what we are sending up, assuming we can cut a deal with whoever is launching today," Sinclair said.

After a long pause, Jack asked, "Do you mean from anywhere? Russia? China? Cause I'm sure there are many launches. If you mean from here, Kennedy Space Center, there is only one launch ready to go, and I hate that fucker. I won't work with him."

"It needs to go from here. We have the equipment here. Jack, please talk to him. Make the arrangement to get it to the space station today. It's a matter of life and death," Sinclair said.

Kate and Jo-Ellen looked at Jack on the screen, shaking their heads in agreement.

"I'm sorry, Jack, but we have no time for games," Sinclair implored. "We need this tech up now! Please reach out to your colleague and get us a ride today. Lives are at stake. You can have the tech when the mission is complete."

"Let me see what I can do," Jack said and hung up.

Otter and a couple of his colleagues were watching the exchange from the other screen. Otter said, "It's not ready. There's a very good chance it won't work. The laser might not be strong enough to pulverize, and we might not be able to aim. We could make things worse; it's very high risk and could put the station in jeopardy!"

"Is there a chance the prototype will explode like during the launch or is the equipment stable?" Kate asked.

"Stable," Sinclair and Otter said at the same time.

"Who on the Space Station will accept and use it?" Kate continued questioning.

"Good point. Someone will need to receive it and set it up. It will work remotely," Sinclair said.

"That does complicate things. Lots of eyes on it. Once we hear back from Jack, we can call NASA and speak to someone on the station," Jo-Ellen said.

"Bloody hell, Yanks, I appreciate the innovation, optimism, and go-get-him attitude, but this is a prototype with tech we don't understand. I don't think it will work! It might hit a few big pieces or it might cause more deadly problems," Otter urged, expressing his concerns again.

"On paper, it should work," Sinclair said. "That has to be enough."

FORTY-ONE

Fifty-Four Days After the Shooting

"The Boston wanker is not launching today. He wanted to go along for the ride or something and it caused delays. I think he wanted it to be a big surprise. The first CEO at the International Space Station. He's a wicked prick," Jack said dramatically, faking a terrible Boston accent.

"That sucks," Kate said. "How long is the delay?"

"Don't know for sure. Could be a couple of days, maybe more. When I heard of the delays, I didn't ask if they would take it. Didn't want to inspire unwanted curiosity in my new tech," Jack added.

"So, nothing is going to the Space Station today or tomorrow?" Sinclair asked.

"Correct, dude. Sorry," Jack said. "Only thing going up is a satellite. If the weather holds, the cattle rancher douche bag is taking it up at dawn. I'm not sure whose satellite it is."

Everyone was quiet for a couple of minutes, considering what to do.

"Sinclair, Jo-Ellen, come here," Kate said, indicating they follow her. She walked them to the far back of the lab where she had found the couch, and they all sat down.

"Maybe we're overthinking this. Why does it have to go to the Space Station? I think if we just get it up there, Rex can take control and make it work. That is if Rex is willing to do this. We still have no idea if he will since he never actually agreed. If he is inclined, what difference does it make where it is, as long as it's in space? And it's human-made technology, well some of it at least. Oh my god, this could be perfect! Send it up on the satellite, and Rex can pulverize everything with it; we don't need to involve any astronauts," Kate whispered, even though they were far from the monitors. She did not want Jack or Otter to hear.

"Excellent point. It's not doing any good sitting here. We just need it in space," Sinclair said. "Let me ask Jack to make a deal and get it on that satellite."

"Or even just on what is taking the satellite up; we just need it up there," Jo-Ellen added.

Sinclair went off to talk to Jack.

Jo-Ellen indicated to Kate to stay on the couch. As soon as Sinclair was out of earshot, she whispered to Kate, "How will you tell Rex about the plan?"

"I don't think we need to tell him. I think he knows what he needs to know. We get it launched, and he either engages or he doesn't. We sure as hell can't make him," Kate said. She did not tell Jo-Ellen that Rex read energy.

An hour later, Jack appeared on the monitor, clearly agitated, explaining the situation. "That rich fucking cowboy bastard. He said that they might accommodate us for $50,000,000! In his greedy-ass dreams! Jesus, it's not a human; it's not even very heavy. He said, 'The satellite is valuable.' Whatever, dude. No way I'm paying him that."

Kate felt her blood boil. Both of these rich assholes were a huge part of the problem, and they were going to be part of the solution whether they liked it or not.

"Yes, you will, Jack!" she said loudly, glancing at Sinclair, whose lips were breaking into a subtle smile. "You must! You helped create all this garbage, this dangerous pollution in space. We don't have time to negotiate. We don't have any other options. The existence of life as we know it on Earth could be at stake. You have billions of dollars, more than you could ever spend in multiple lifetimes. Call him and agree; find out where we need to take this equipment. Now!"

Kate had never spoken directly to Jack, and he seemed startled by her determination.

Kate took a deep breath, waiting for Jack to respond, but he didn't say a word.

"Jack, Rex killed 70,000,000 Americans in a matter of a few minutes. You were very lucky you were not with your gun! Your luck might run out, and our only hope to prevent more mass violence is to get this equipment into outer space. Call him back now. If he launches at dawn, we could have this equipment to Rex in a few hours. We have no idea when the next opportunity will arise. Call him back now!" Kate shouted.

Jack stared at Kate for a few seconds and then hung up.

"Where does the cattle kingpin launch? Which pad?" Kate asked.

A few calls later and they knew where they were heading.

Jack's staff drove them in the fancy trucks to the hangar where they were preparing for the launch. They also pushed the cart with the final product slowly behind as Kate, Sinclair, and Jo-Ellen rushed into the hangar.

They explained the situation to the head engineer. "We need our equipment to go up with the satellite. We need to attach it to the rocket taking the satellite up," Sinclair said. "It's very important, so it needs to be well secured."

"Okay, right," the engineer responded with a cocked head. "Hey, are you Kate Stellute, the person of interest in the mass shooting?" he asked, his voice high with concern.

Kate was surprised he recognized her, but then realized she wasn't wearing a mask. Her fear of the virus was dwarfed by Rex's threat of more global violence.

"Yes, but that shouldn't matter; we need this in space at dawn," Kate replied.

"I have no idea what you are talking about. We are extremely busy, so please leave. I'm not even sure how you got in here, but I'm calling security," the engineer said, reaching for his phone.

"I am security," Jo-Ellen said, flashing her Space Force badge, "and he works for NASA."

"I don't care. My boss pays a shitload of money to lease this space and the launch pad when needed. Go away now!" the engineer snapped, before being distracted by his ringing phone.

"Hello," he said, turning his back to them and walking away.

Kate, Sinclair, and Jo-Ellen started to slowly walk toward the door of the hangar. Just as they reached it, the engineer called out to them.

"Hey, stop! Okay, we'll send it up with the satellite. Let my staff take it so we can figure out how," the engineer said.

"Guess we know who was on the phone," Jo-Ellen said, watching the engineer and his staff take the laser away.

"We can't let it out of our sight; we need to see it be placed on the satellite to be sure it goes up," Sinclair said.

"Good thinking," Jo-Ellen said.

All three rushed to follow the laser prototype.

FORTY-TWO

Fifty-Five Days After the Shooting

A few minutes later, the head engineer approached Kate, Sinclair, and Jo-Ellen.

"Bad news: The laser is too heavy for the rocket. Even though your equipment isn't very heavy, it's too much for this launch. Many variables would have to be changed to make it work, including altering the payload adapter. Adding your equipment could affect the release of the satellite and damage it. We don't have time to make the necessary changes," he said. "I'm sure my boss will not be pleased either."

"Oh no! So that's it? We can't get this up?" Kate asked. "No. That's not acceptable. We have to get it up there now!"

"Sorry, there is nothing we can do," the head engineer said, then quickly walked away.

"We will think of something, Kate," Sinclair said "We need to look into what is going up next, tomorrow or the day after. We're not giving up."

"Call Jack," Jo-Ellen said. "I have an idea. Get him on the phone."

Sinclair called Jack, and he picked up immediately.

"What's going on? I'm on my way to the hangar; be there in a few minutes. If they won't let me in, I'll meet you at the pad. That douche doesn't like me near his equipment, but he likes my money…" Jack said before Jo-Ellen cut him off.

"Shut up. The laser equipment is too heavy for the rocket, and there isn't enough time to make the needed adjustments," Jo-Ellen explained quickly.

"Oh, that sucks. It makes sense, but it sucks," Jack said, sounding disappointed. "I guess the bright side is I saved a lot of money."

"Nope, you are not saving any money. You will ask them to take the satellite off the rocket, put our equipment on, and launch at dawn. There are delays all the time. They will have to send the satellite up on another launch. Call the cattle guy and tell him you will pay for whatever penalties or problems this causes for him. Call him now! People's lives are in danger!" Jo-Ellen shouted into the phone.

"No way. He will know I'm desperate and charge me a buttload more! No way!" Jack whined.

"Call him now and pay whatever it takes. We don't have time to fuck around," Jo-Ellen said, motioning for Sinclair to end the call.

"Jo-Ellen, you are brilliant!" Kate said.

"Do you think it will work? They'll still have to make significant weight adjustments in a short time," Sinclair said.

"Come on, let's find out," Jo-Ellen said, chasing after the head engineer.

They stayed in the hangar most of the night, watching the engineers prepare. They seemed to see the sudden change as an exciting challenge and rose to the occasion.

Kate, Sinclair, and Jo-Ellen joined them as they moved to the launch pad without the satellite just after midnight. Jack was there when they arrived.

"You bet your asses I'm going to watch my money go up," Jack said. "I can't believe I have to pay that asshole $100,000,000!"

They all stood at a safe distance and watched the launch just before six a.m.

When the rocket disappeared from sight, Jo-Ellen asked, "Now what?"

"We wait to see if Rex uses it," Kate replied, staring up at the sky.

"Let's go to the HQ building. If things are being pulverized, NASA will be watching," Sinclair said.

Thirty minutes later, they were in the historic viewing room watching monitors flash different scenes from various satellites and the Space Station. Jack was pacing, occasionally bothering engineers with stupid comments or jokes. On the monitors, everything seemed calm, quiet, cold, and dark; it was space.

"It does seem too vast to ruin," Kate said to Sinclair. "It seems huge. Endless. Mysterious."

"Course that is what White Europeans thought of Africa and America. Hell, it's what we think about the oceans today, as we use them as huge garbage cans," Sinclair said. "What's the old saying? *The solution to pollution is dilution.* Total bullshit nowadays."

"True. The size allows us to justify our behavior. We are just one little consumer, one little Earthling. How much damage can we do?" Kate said sarcastically. "I mean, climate change will impact hundreds of millions of lives. Kill people. There will be accountability. I guess there is karma," Kate said, mumbling quietly.

"You okay?" Sinclair asked.

"Just exhausted and hungry. But mostly exhausted," Kate said, sliding down in a chair. She put her head back and closed her eyes.

A few minutes later, the room started to hum. People were calling to each other and changing monitor images. Kate snapped awake and asked, "What's happening?"

Jo-Ellen was waving them over to where she was sitting at a computer.

"I've been randomly checking in on pieces of debris, scrolling through the database, pinpointing their coordinates, and checking if we have eyes nearby. A few were missing, but I thought that could easily be a glitch; things can move. Now, it seems many are missing! Look! Let's find the broken satellites, for example," she said, typing away. Look up there," Jo-Ellen said, pointing to a monitor. "Gone!"

"Are you seeing any new collisions? Are we creating new debris?" Sinclair asked in a loud whisper.

"Not yet," Jo-Ellen said. "All the defunct satellites are gone, and they are huge; if they aren't creating more debris, we might be okay!"

They kept watching Jo-Ellen's database and the monitors. The other staff around them started to realize what was happening but had no idea why.

"Did the Russians or Chinese figure out how to pulverize debris?" Kate heard an engineer ask from across the room while staring at the screens. "Whose tech is this?"

All eyes turned to Jack. He shrugged, a cocky smirk on his face.

More people came into the room, including Space Force staff. The acting general was speaking to NASA leadership. Everyone was trying to be the first to figure out what was happening. Agents were scrambling, requesting to speak with representatives from the Israel Space Agency, Roscosmos, and CNSA.

For an hour, Kate watched the screens and monitors, listening to the chatter and enjoying the exciting energy pulsing through the room.

At times, the buzz sounded stressful and scary as people expressed concerns that important technology had been pulverized. Then relieved shouts of, "No, wait, we located it!" would recalibrate the vibe back to giddy excitement.

We might have actually done it! Thank you, Rex!

"The world is aware. Social media is blowing up; *#NASASocial* is trending! Space.com is buzzing with speculation about what is happening!" an excited young staffer yelled to everyone in the room.

"Let's get out of here before anyone starts asking questions," Kate said to Sinclair as things seem to be winding down. "I'm starving and really, really tired."

"Okay. It looks like the show is almost over. Jo-Ellen, let us know if anything changes," Sinclair said, taking Kate's hand.

"If it keeps going at this pace, I doubt there will be any debris left by the time you walk out of the building. I mean, it seems to be done now. Just like that. It's amazing!" Jo-Ellen was smiling as she spoke, still staring at her computer screen.

Are those tears in Jo-Ellen's eyes? Look like happy tears to me!

Kate and Sinclair walked out through the huge, quiet halls of Kennedy Space Center Headquarters. They made the long walk back to the hangar, watching birds and wildlife stir in the early morning before it got too hot. They were still holding hands.

Kate's body tingled all over, pure electricity.

Is this from our success or from touching Sinclair?

"We need to watch out for alligators; they cross the roads sometimes," Kate said as they walked along.

As they approached the hangar which contained the debris from the collision, they saw it. Far across the large empty parking lot, sitting all alone, was Karisma's white CR-V.

FORTY-THREE

Fifty-Five Days After
the Shooting

W hen they got back to Karisma's rental place, Kate showered, ate some fast food they picked up on the way, and then slept for several hours. It was late afternoon when she woke up, dressed, and went to find Sinclair. He was in the living room, staring at the TV.

"It's all over the news. They are interviewing NASA officials, astronauts, Space Force agents, engineers from all over the world, and, of course, Jack. They're all trying to figure out who did this and why. Generally, it's very celebratory. I'm not sure the average American, or world citizen, understands the significance, but the astronauts, engineers, and people in the biz sure do," Sinclair said. "If Rex's boss accepts this as enough, you have saved the world in multiple ways, Kate."

Kate smiled, sat down on the couch, and continued watching the news for a few minutes.

"It's so strange seeing hope and happiness on CNN. Let's just enjoy this moment," she said.

They cut from a giggly NASA engineer explaining how significant this was to making space travel safer for all mankind to a desk anchor who said, "The President is going to make a statement."

His face suddenly appeared on the screen, looking dour as usual. Kate thought he was a humorless, cruel, and angry man before the mass shooting, and since he lost his kids, his rancor and conspiracies seemed even darker. "We don't know who has pulverized the space debris, including dozens of satellites. We sure hope they weren't ours or important since they are very, very expensive. And with satellites, not everyone knows whose are whose or what they are really for."

"Yes, we do. NASA knows all that, and they told you that the ones destroyed were defunct, you lying piece of shit," Sinclair said to the TV.

"I have the Department of Defense and Space Force looking into this. We must find out exactly what happened. Aren't you all happy now that I created Space Force? If this was a hostile act, we need to know. Some say we don't have the technology to do this. However, if space is truly safer now, and it did happen from Kennedy Space Center, my Administration takes full credit. America is number one under my leadership and investment in NASA and space," the President added.

Kate turned off the TV and said, "I can't watch it. He's not making any sense. Something wonderful happened, and I can't let that man mess with my relief and happiness right now. By the end of the day, he may convince half of America that the other half of America did it to somehow hurt them. I really can't take it."

"Let's get out of here," Sinclair said. "Let's go to Karisma's restaurant. They don't open on Sunday nights now, but she invites friends and family over and does a Sunday family dinner. We deserve some drinks and celebration!" Sinclair said, holding out his hand to pull Kate off the couch.

A couple of hours later, with a full belly, Kate was swigging beer and watching the ocean. She was on the deck at Karisma's restaurant, safely social distancing. She was listening to Anton and Harriet tell their friends and cousins a hilarious story about church that morning. They both tried to best each other at mimicking the walk and talk of a preacher. She was laughing along with everyone else. It was great hearing people talk about things besides COVID, guns, pollution, and violence.

She watched Sinclair across the deck as he laughed with Nancy and Karisma. They would occasionally toast and hug. Kate assumed they were having an intimate wake for Yvette and Larry, and she had no intention of interfering.

He is extremely handsome, with that smile, those eyes. If the world was saved, it was just as much due to his efforts as mine.

Her phone rang. Kate walked a little way down the beach to answer and speak with her mother.

"I saw it on the news! The garbage in space has been pulverized by some new laser! I don't understand it, but I know that it was you and Sinclair making the world safer. Kate, I am so proud of you," her mom squealed with relief and joy.

"And a whole lot of help from Claudia, Jo-Ellen, Otter, Jack, and Rex," Kate said, smiling. "We are at Karisma's restaurant celebrating. We have to hope it was enough; we don't know for sure yet."

"Stay in Florida!" Kate's mom exclaimed loudly. "I'm heading home tomorrow. Without the kids, it will be a straight shot. Come and stay with me for a few days? I would love that! I want to hear all the details when you are not in the middle of a well-deserved celebration. Sinclair is more than welcome to join us. I can't wait to meet him."

Kate glanced at Sinclair, who seemed to feel her eyes on him and turned to look at her, giving her a slow smile and a wink. Her stomach dive-bombed, and she forgot for a second that she was talking to her mother.

"Kate? You there?" her mom asked.

"Yeah, Mom, I'm here. I can't wait for you to meet Sinclair either," Kate said, smiling.

FORTY-FOUR

Fifty-Seven Days After the Shooting

K ate and Sinclair stayed at Karisma's for a couple more nights. Jo-Ellen came by to report that no one could figure out how it happened.

"Otter and Jack are arguing over who owns the equipment, the new technology. Space Force also claimed it was theirs since some parts were taken from their hangar. It doesn't matter. When they get it back down, they will realize it didn't actually work. Though they have all the specs, and I am sure they will try to make another one," Jo-Ellen said.

"Well, they will need to figure it out fast, or this whole nightmare was for nothing. They will just create more debris and garbage, and the violence could still happen," Kate said. "We don't know if we are in the clear or if this was acceptable to the others."

"All we can do is hope for the best. I'm heading back to D.C. tomorrow. Will you promise to call me if you hear from Rex? Any sign at all, okay? I would prefer we work together like we have been, as a team. I really hated following you two," Jo-Ellen said, smiling.

"Jo-Ellen, am I still a person of interest regarding the mass shooting? I realize Space Force has gone quiet regarding me and Rex in the media. Is that a permanent situation?" Kate asked. "There is no more reason to follow me, right?"

"Space Force knows what happened. You are a hero. They better not bother you about anything ever again, but let me check in and get back to you," Jo-Ellen said, no longer smiling.

FORTY-FIVE

Fifty-Eight Days After the Shooting

Kate and Sinclair drove to her mom's town and stayed at her condo. They enjoyed telling her all the details and drama of the past few weeks. Kate thought that since Sinclair, her mom, and Jo-Ellen were the only people on the planet that knew everything, they should talk it into the ground before they returned to D.C.; they would have to act like none of it happened once they got home.

"I am going to have to write this down. I need to keep track of exactly who knows what and why, or I will trip up," Kate told Sinclair with a deep sigh as they walked the beach at sunset, holding hands. "I'm not good with lying, and I dread talking to Kyle. I guess he's the only real problem. What am I going to say to him?"

"You will know what to say when you see him. You are a brilliant, caring, kind, and yes, brave person. Just say what comes naturally. Hell, Rex picked you out of everyone left on Earth. You handled Rex, a major crisis, and may have saved the world. Don't stress over it; you will know what to say," Sinclair said, kissing Kate's hand.

"Every day that goes by, I feel more like it worked," Kate said at dinner. "Every little thing is gonna be alright," Kate and her mom sang together, and Sinclair joined in.

Later, while alone in the kitchen doing the dishes, Kate's mom whispered, "I adore Sinclair."

"Me too," Kate replied.

FORTY-SIX

Fifty-Nine Days After
the Shooting

Kate was eager for a good run on the beach before it got too hot. They planned to drive back to D.C. the next day, and she was already missing Florida. She was listening to the waves and watching birds fly out of her path as she started to jog. Kate hoped to spot some dolphins.

She barely set out when she felt that horrid roller coaster feeling; before she knew it, she hit the floor hard in the white room. On her hands and knees, she threw up the coffee and water she had for breakfast.

"God dammit, Rex!" she yelled as soon as she could speak. She moved away from the puke, sitting crossed-legged on the floor, rubbing her arms and legs hard, trying to warm up fast.

"Did it work?" she asked through chattering teeth.

Rex did not respond, and Kate stood as soon as she was warm enough.

"Well? Did it work?" she asked again.

"I am not sure," Rex said in his slow, careful speech. "I told them the debris and dangerous garbage were removed. I told them the humans sent something into space and pulverized all of it. Others would be safe traveling nearby."

"Okay. Good. That is what needed to happen, right?" Kate said.

Rex did not reply for several minutes, and Kate became concerned.

"Rex, you said they were angry about the collision, and we needed to get rid of the dangerous pollution by working together; we did just that. We found a loophole. Are you worried they didn't buy it?" Kate asked.

"I told them. They seemed to accept it, but they are coming anyway," Rex said.

"Why? To do more violence?" Kate asked, her voice rising in fear.

"I don't know," Rex replied.

"Do they do this type of thing often?" Kate asked.

"No, they were doing their work, just as I was doing mine. I have never had anyone come and check on my work. They might be concerned," Rex replied slowly.

"Why are they concerned?" Kate asked.

"I have stayed here a long time," Rex replied slowly.

"Not that long. The collision was just over a year ago. The shooting was only eight weeks ago. That's not long at all." Kate did not understand and had a sinking feeling in her stomach.

Have we actually done what happens in almost every movie ever made? Did we celebrate too soon?

"Those VIPs must have been very special. Did you just happen to be nearby?" Kate asked, realizing how lucky everyone was that Rex came. Things could have been worse, but she wanted to understand more about the timeline that Rex and the others were focused on.

"I was near, but others were close as well. They were very important to us. Their work, their morals, their vision. Many wanted to come. They still want to come," Rex said slowly and then paused for several seconds.

"Why did you come, Rex?" Kate asked.

"I came because I was nearby, but also because of our relationship. The ones who were killed, you would call them my parents," Rex said.

The End Of Book Two Of The Impact Series

QUESTIONS AND TOPICS FOR DISCUSSION

1. In what ways does Kate's character or personality change between *The Shooting* and *The Collision*? Why do you think this happens?

2. How aware of space debris were you before reading *The Collision*? Did you know how dangerous it is? Has this story motivated you to find out more?

3. What are some of the parallels between pollution in space and pollution on Earth?

4. What characters do you like most and least in *The Collision*? Why?

5. Kate is made the scapegoat by many people. Name some of them and why you think they are so quick to blame her.

6. Gun violence has been declared a public health crisis in the United States. Does the author explore this issue in a satisfying way? Why or why not?

7. How do Kate and Sinclair and Kate and Rex's relationship evolve between *The Shooting* and *The Collision*?

8. What do you think it means to be brave? Is Kate brave? How about Sinclair and Kyle?

9. Kate often says she would not want to live in a world that does not include several things that are important to her. What are some things you value as highly in your world?

10. What does Rex represent to you?

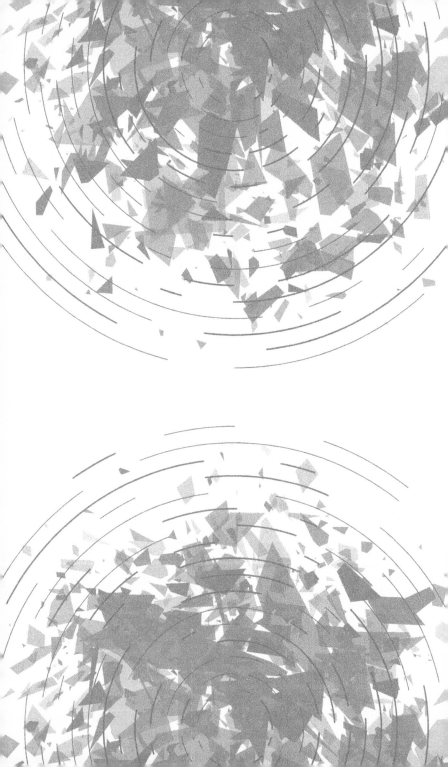

AUTHOR BIO

C K Westbrook is an environmentalist who lives and works in Washington D.C. and is a self-described old-school news junkie. Since the state of our planet and the news are bleak and depressing, Westbrook escapes reality by creating intriguing characters in a science fiction world. The world these characters live in may also be dark and scary, but they do have fantastic adventures that impact their planet. In addition to creating imaginative stories, Westbrook literally breaks free from daily life with an intense passion for travel and has been to all seven continents. Westbrook loves weaving real-world topics and crises into suspenseful sci-fi and fantasy. To learn more about CK Westbrook, please go to www.ckwestbrook.com.

Ready for more Kate, Sinclair, and Kyle action and suspense? *The Judgment,* book three of The Impact Series, will be published in winter 2023.

More books from
4 Horsemen Publications

Horror, Thriller, & Suspense

Alan Berkshire
Jungle

Amanda Byrd
Trapped
Moratorium
Medicate

Erika Lance
Jimmy
Illusions of Happiness
No Place for Happiness
I Hunt You

Maria DeVivo
Witch of the Black Circle
Witch of the Red Thorn

Mark Tarrant
The Mighty Hook
The Death Riders
Howl of the Windigo
Guts and Garter Belts

Fantasy & SciFi

Brandon Hill & Terence Pegasus
Between the Devil and the Dark

C.K. Westbrook
The Shooting
The Collision

Ty Carlson
The Bench
The Favorite

D. Lambert
To Walk into the Sands
Rydan
Celebrant
Northlander
Esparan
King
Traitor
His Last Name

Discover more at
4HorsemenPublications.com